I0694115

Annemarie Nikolaus

The Granddaughter

Quick, quick, slow – Lietzensee Dance Club

Novel

1

"Forward – forward – side – together..." The bright voice of Ines Grube covered the music. Nine couples struggled to follow the coach's instructions.

Madeline Lagrange planted her arm against her dance partner's chest to create more distance. "Robert, you're gonna crush me!"

Robert Merck pursed his lips, but he loosened his grip. "Better now?" His voice was full of mockery. "I didn't know you were so fragile."

She rolled her eyes. At that she promptly got out of step; Robert gripped her more firmly again.

As they danced past the open door, she took a look at the big clock above the bar. It seemed to have stopped in the meantime. Shouldn't the lesson be over any second?

Grandpa were sitting at the counter and appeared to be watching her; his feet were moving in time. Even after almost twenty years he hadn't forgotten anything. Maybe she should practice with him instead of that annoying guy.

Ines turned off the music and ordered to take a short break.

"Good grief!" With the back of her hand Madeline wiped the sweat off her forehead. Then she looked at her feet. "My new stockings might be ruined."

"But if you always put your feet under mine."

"Oh, that's right!" Did he think that was funny? She left Robert and went to the bar.

"My Madeline!" With radiant eyes George Lagrange held a glass of mineral water to her. "You're far better than your partner. Who is he anyway?"

Marga Fischer, who looked after both the office and the counter, reached for George's empty glass, the bottle of red wine in the other hand for a refill. "Your granddaughter has rhythm in her blood. Who might she have inherited it from?" With a twinkle in her eye she replenished his glass.

"Certainly not from my son. He just blew up half the lab once again."

Marga stared at him in dismay. "No!" She laughed nervously. "You're just making fun of me again!"

"Not at all. It was in the papers yesterday." A frown line appeared on his forehead. "Of course, he didn't tell me." He took his glass off Marga and turned back to Madeline. "So who's the one you're dancing with?"

She shrugged. "Robert Merck. I think, his father's a colleague of Klaus Wächter."

"Cop family then." The frown on George's forehead disappeared. When Robert came to the counter right afterwards, he looked at the young man with a friendly smile.

Robert ordered a beer from Marga. "I've earned that now."

"What about driving?" Madeline pointedly asked. "You promised to take me home."

He blushed to the tips of his hair. Madeline hid her amusement behind her raised glass.

George thoughtfully scratched his chin. "Will you continue dancing with us after the try-out course?"

Robert's gaze went to Madeline: "The Lietzensee Dance Club has a remarkable reputation; I like that very much. I think so – if I can find a partner for the dance group?"

"Certainly." George nodded contentedly. "Well, here's to a

good time." He held up his glass to Robert. "I've just been watching you."

"So? What do you think?" Robert was tensing. "May I hope to be perfect someday?"

"Ugh!" Madeline snorted. "What is it with you? Fishing for compliments, Robert?" She made no effort to hide her contempt.

"You have no sense of humor today, Madeline! I didn't step on your foot that many times!"

George followed Madeline's instinctive gaze downwards. She had a stain on her right foot next to her ankle. "Dancing in sandals isn't very smart. Get yourself some real dancing shoes."

"What for? Once I cross the street in them, I can throw them away."

"What do you professionally do, Robert?"

"Nothing much." He shrugged. "District office Reinickendorf. But certainly not for the rest of my life." A sparkle came into his eyes. "A career as a ballroom dancer... That'll get you thinking."

"I was quite successful in my time. Four times in the top three of the German Championship; also twice at the World Championships." But Grandpa never won; that was something he always kept from the young people. "My father had been involved already in the early days of formation dancing before World War II. Madeline continues the family tradition."

What came to his mind? "Grandpa!" Madeline shook her head. "To get a place in medicine at the university, I know already now what will fill my days up to graduation."

"But you're so smart, Madeline. I can't imagine you need so much time to study." Robert reached for her hand. "The lesson resumes."

"I'm gonna finish my water." Madeline withdrew her hand and waved him towards the dance hall. "Go on, go on."

Robert looked hesitantly back and forth between Madeline and the dance hall. Then the music started softly; Ines would continue in a moment. He started to move, still hesitant.

"Whew!" Madeline sighed when he was out of earshot. "He. Gets. On. My. Nerves."

"But why? He's nice, isn't he? And so ambitious."

"He's just not my type."

George grinned. "And who's your type?"

She looked dreamily at the ceiling. "Tall, slender, black-haired. Adult.

"That sounds like you had someone in particular in mind. Do you have a crush on one of your teachers?"

Madeline laughed; that was none of Grandpa's business. "I'll be going."

After two steps, however, she stopped. Holding her breath, she stared at the man who were just walking in. Slim and broad-shouldered; jeans and t-shirt so tight that the movements of his muscles underneath were visible. And black hair, albeit a little too short for her taste. "Wow!" She exhaled slowly. Did she just conjure him up?

Still looking at the man from the corner of her eye, she turned to Marga. "Who's that guy?"

"Chris Rinehart, our caller!"

"Oh?" What was that supposed to mean?

"Madeline!" Robert waved fiercely and with a sigh she started moving again.

***

Chris' gaze became stuck on Madeline, who strutted to the dance hall with obvious displeasure. Her pretty face was frozen in a dark grimace. What was the girl doing here if she didn't feel like dancing?

"Good evening, Chris!" Marga tore him from his contemplations. "I've arranged for a replacement. The equipment could no longer be repaired."

George raised his eyebrows. "Replacement, Marga? That's not scheduled in our budget."

"Neither is repair. But that's all right. I talked to Werner."

George's forehead smoothed a little. "You always think of everything."

Marga quickly lowered her head over the sink and put the empty glasses in it. George strolled to the dance hall. Chris joined him and leaned into the door frame.

Most couples still displayed a rather pitiful picture. And what Madeline was doing with her partner looked more like a wrestling match than a slow waltz. Why didn't she leave the lead to him as it should be? Obviously, this wasn't her thing.

Their glances met; spontaneously Chris smiled at her. She blushed and quickly looked away. Chris didn't want to look away. The wine-red streak in her disheveled dark blond hair gave her something daring that attracted him. It fit the skirmish with her partner.

"The course could extend one night and I'll show them some square dance steps," he told George.

George stiffened. "This is a try-out course in ballroom dancing!" He cleared his throat and afterwards his voice sounded less harsh. "It's trouble enough for a club to run a course at all."

Marga rolled her eyes; thereupon Chris refrained from replying.

2

At the next meal together with the family, George had of course raved how proud he would be to have another professional ballroom dancer in his family. Madeline's mother Konstanze reminded him that Madeline now had to study for her *Abitur*; that one he could accept. He was a little offended though, when Madeline declared that she was learning to dance only for "domestic use": As a future doctor, she should just be able to dance. Therefore she comforted him with the promise to continue dancing in the dance circle after the course. She'd certainly get rid of Robert somehow.

On Friday, however, she was still sitting at her desk in the late afternoon studying for a test. Eventually she got stuck on the pages of "PloS One" in the latest medical articles. Research would actually be an exciting alternative to foreign assignments with *"Médecins Sans Frontières"*. Instead of looking at the computer screen, she thoughtfully stared at the Africa posters on the wall.

"Madeline, telephone!" Konstanze tore her from her thoughts.

She jumped down the stairs; Konstanze held the receiver to her.

"Did you turn off your cell?" Robert's voice sounded angry.

"Yeah, sure. I'm cramming."

"Do you know what time it is?"

She looked at her wrist watch. "It really wasn't necessary to call to ask me that!"

As Robert exploded, she held the receiver far away and rolled her eyes.

"Why didn't you just cancel on him?" exclaimed Konstanze from the kitchen.

Madeline sighed and put her hand on the receiver. "Grandpa would be disappointed, *Maman*." – She turned back to the phone. "Listen, Robert. If you want me to get going, just restrain yourself."

"Of course I want you to come. Take a cab so you'll be on time. I'll pay."

God help him, he said one word when she arrived.

Robert was waiting for her at the bar; he had cooled off meanwhile. "Marga, may I have a beer for me and Madeline?"

"Robert, you're out of your mind." Madeline left him.

In the small dance hall a couple stood at the window and talked quietly. Following her experience in the course Madeline introduced herself only with her first name.

The girl shook her hand. "I'm Tanja and this is my brother Axel. He's my partner here in the dance circle." Partner? Madeline scrutinized them suspiciously. Wasn't this just like the disco? What a bummer.

Robert came to the door of the hall with his can. "Now, did you want your beer or not?"

"No, thanks. No beer breath."

For a moment he looked like being scolded; then he placed his beer with a shrug next to the music equipment. But he had already been drinking. When he took her by the hand for the first dance, the stale smell drifted to her.

Robert moved so close during the slow waltz that his lips

almost touched her ear. At least her ears couldn't smell his beer-fed breath.

Then he stepped on her foot with full force. "We really should take your grandfather's offer and let him train us."

"I don't have time," she hissed in a voice filled with pain. "I have to study."

"Once a week. Come on, agree."

"This here is once a week, Robert."

The music was dying down; Ines approached them. "Madeline, leave your partner to me for a minute."

And with pleasure! Ines took the lead and made sure that he kept his head in the right place.

However, he did not take it to heart; afterwards he glued himself to Madeline again. Her hopeful look at the clock after each round was soon blocked by dancers gathering at the bar. Resignedly she kept dancing.

By the end of the dance circle, the place in front of the counter had become so crowded that she could barely get through. A lanky blond guy suddenly took a step backwards and Madeline kicked him in the heels.

"Pardon me!"

He turned around and she looked into two cheerful grey-blue eyes. "Awesome performance! A woman kicking me from behind rarely happens to me!" He grabbed her by the hips with both hands. "I'd love to dance with you some day!" He pushed her past him.

At first she wanted to respond indignantly to this hit on, but his laughter reconciled her with him. "Would you like to sign up already for the Carnival ball?" She'd rather dance with just about anyone than with Robert.

"That's too far away!" He still had a smile on his face. He pushed her one step further and then let her go.

"Try hibernation," she retorted.

He bent to her ear and whispered: "Don't tell anyone. I've got better plans for the winter."

She smirked. "Without me? Then what are you complaining about?"

"What other choice do I have? I'm going to Singapore next week." He laughed at her flabbergasted mien.

Singapore! What a kid he was! He didn't look like he could afford it. Still laughing she left the club's rooms. Whatever — in any case, she was meeting nice people. A broad-shouldered figure with black hair invaded her thoughts.

3

As if he didn't trust her an inch, George showed up on Friday afternoon after the Christmas break and then took Madeline to the dance circle.

Slowly he crept across the icy roads to the club. "Ines told me you don't get along with Robert. Are you wrestling with him for the lead?"

"He wrestles with me!" Hopefully he realized she didn't want to talk about Robert.

"He's a nice guy!"

"Is there someone at the club who isn't nice?"

He laughed. "Sometimes! But they don't last long."

He looked at her boots as he opened the door for her to get out. "Did you bring again only sandals to change?"

"I don't own any other high heels."

"Even in flat shoes, you're not too small for Robert."

"Maybe I'll dance with someone else someday." She stomped after him through the snow, swinging the gym bag with the sandals.

At six o'clock on the dot, they entered the club rooms. Robert hasn't come yet. Others were also missing; the weather might be to blame. Maybe this was a chance to catch another dancer.

"How strict are the mores here, Grandpa? If someone is late..."

He laughed. "We're careful not to discipline the folk attending the dance circle. It's hard enough to keep the number of members stable."

She linked arms with him. "I didn't know the club had a problem."

"Well, he hasn't. No more than any other dance club."

"I get it... If everyone thinks like me: dance lessons are necessary to avoid embarrassment. But then..."

George's face darkened. Was he still hoping she would get involved with the club?

Ines came up to her from the office. "Madeline? Robert's not coming today. I got you a guest dancer." She pointed to the dance hall. At the stereo, with his back to her, stood a lanky man with blond hair.

"You see, Grandpa. For this one I need high heels."

Heels! Wasn't that the guy she kicked the other day? Whoever he was, at least he wasn't Robert.

She followed Ines and the man at the stereo turned around. Indeed.

"Who's that?" she whispered to Ines.

"Hinnerk Martens. Studies geology or geography. Something like that."

His amused smile indicated that he recognized Madeline. "Hello, Ines, is she the poor girl who has to dance with me tonight?"

"Madeline has started dancing with the last try-out course. So be lenient."

"As if I could do a lot better here." Mischief glittered in his eyes. "We'll figure it out."

"I already know I'm going to enjoy dancing with you." She laughed to him. "You don't complain about kicks."

He linked arms with her. "Maybe I'm working on a revenge. Today Ines has tango on the agenda. That would be ideal."

"For a kick from behind?"

"For a kick from behind."

"Then I have to disappoint you: We haven't learned these complicated moves yet."

"Kicking is quite uncomplicated."

The first dance, though, was a slow waltz. Hinnerk had a soft grip, correct on her shoulder blade. After two minutes she understood his signals and relaxed. "I knew it would be fun."

He laughed and lead her into a sideways movement. "You dance pretty good for a beginner. Talented."

"Why did Ines say you were temporary?"

Hinnerk shrugged. "Maybe because I step in when I have time? When I'm in Berlin."

"Don't you live here?"

"I even study here. But I often work abroad."

"And that works?"

"It's even a stroke of luck. I'm gaining experience in my field of study and may already have a job for later." He grinned. Why had he noticed she hadn't believed him? "I really was in Singapore for the Christmas holidays. Geological surveys for a new airport site."

At the end of the slow waltz, Ines nodded appreciatively to Madeline. Hopefully she wouldn't take it straight away to Grandpa.

Hinnerk entertained her for the remaining time of the dance circle with anecdotes from his foreign assignments. Unlike Robert, he didn't care in which light he appeared. He had no problem admitting mistakes. Of course, he was just a student, while Robert had completed his formation and had a proper administrative position.

She liked Hinnerk more and more and in the end she looked for a spin to continue dancing with him.

"Now I still don't know why you're dancing only as a substitute. You do it so well." Maybe it would help if she flattered him. "Do you lack a steady partner because of your jobs abroad?"

He smirked. "Are you volunteering?" She blushed and again he let mischief dance in his eyes. "You don't have to be embarrassed that you asked." His gaze lit up. "Maybe you'd even be reason enough to make something regular out of it."

"Yes?" She put in her gaze all the expectations she could muster.

He nudged her nose. "Two points speak against that: First, you have a partner."

She made a face.

"I see!" For a moment he looked at her thoughtfully. "Second, these ballroom dances don't really blow my mind. It's too... too..." He shrugged.

"Then why are you doing it?"

"Because I'm a nice person, maybe?" He grinned cheekily.

"You're kidding me!" She stepped on his foot.

"That was on purpose, Madeline. That's not nice of you."

"Maybe because I'm not a nice person." She breathed heavily. "You're in the club for a reason. Why, if you don't like this?"

"Because the club has decided to afford a square dance group, what is very unusual. That is fun!"

Madeline looked at him suspiciously. "Why? What's the difference?"

"I don't know. The people, maybe? The music?" He shrugged again. "Stop by and watch."

Why did he want that? "I don't have time to make the extra trip."

"We dance on Fridays too."

It dawned on her. "Is that why you were here the other day?"

He nodded. "Alternates with Tuesdays. It depends on Chris' shifts." Chris – the gorgeous man she had conjured up... Now it became interesting.

"All those people at the bar?"

"We need a lot of people; otherwise we can't dance." He stopped and looked at her questioningly. "Do you even know what square dancing is?"

"Doesn't everybody know? Occurs in all Western movies."

He looked a little suspicious, but then he settled for her answer. Should she agree to come? In the end, he might misunderstand. If the square dancers were dancing again on a Friday, she'd just stop by.

4

The following Friday she called Ines and asked if Robert had canceled again and if she was dancing with Hinnerk. Ines certainly thought it weird, but she didn't care.

"I'm sorry; he's coming," she got to hear. Ines laughed softly. "I say it in all seriousness, because I've already realized you are not getting along with Robert. – Why don't you tell him you don't want to dance with him?"

"Because then he wouldn't have a partner."

"And change club? Madeline, don't let that become your problem."

She sighed. "I would like to learn more myself. That's why I don't want... to hurt his feelings."

"You can't help it. Sooner or later. Maybe you should get it over with?"

This now became too personal for her; she quickly changed the subject. "So, Hinnerk isn't there tonight."

"Not with us!" Ines suddenly sounded a little sharp; didn't she appreciate Hinnerk then? But maybe she just appreciated his willingness to step in when necessary. Adults just were thinking too complicated.

Madeline went in front of the mirror with two skirts. "Not with us." Which meant Hinnerk would be there when the dance circle ended. She chose the wide swinging silk skirt that reached down her knees.

While she stood in the bathroom tracing her lips with a

contour pencil, Konstanze came up and stopped in the door frame with an astonished look. "You seem to be about to go into battle today." She grinned. "Shall I loan you some of my war paint? I have an eyeliner that goes with that skirt."

She went to the mirror cabinet and looked for the eyeliner without paying attention to Madeline's stuttered answer. Then she sat on the stool and pulled her between her legs. "Close your eyes." The pencil stroked along her eyelash lines. "Open your eyes!" Konstanze contoured the lower edge of the eyes. Then she nodded contentedly. "Now everyone will turn after you. You won't be able to save yourself from dancing partners."

"But, *Maman*! Don't you know we have our permanent partners there?

"Oh, I do! But I also know that you would like to have another partner." She put the eyeliner away. "If you're not having fun, you may as well let it go. In the disco you have just as much exercise."

"If Grandpa could hear you now..."

"... then he would have a heart attack. But he doesn't hear it. That you don't appreciate this Robert is a good reason to stop."

Madeline hugged her. "Thank you for taking my side."

"That's what mothers are for!" A reassuring thought. Konstanze would certainly come up with something to get her out of it without offending Grandpa too much.

The dance circle was complete; again Robert was standing at the bar with a beer in his hand. Immediately, anger rose in Madeline. Was he that stupid or did he consciously ignore that she was disgusted to dance wrapped in beer-fed breath?

With his free hand he reached out to her. "You're even more beautiful tonight than usual. I can't believe it." He drew her closer to him, although she stiffened noticeably.

Buffoon! "Why?" She put on a sugar-sweet smile and clambered onto a barstool. "Am I so unlike myself today? You recognized me after all!"

"I would recognize you anywhere and in any disguise." He pursed his lips. How could a grown man behave like a secondary-school pupil! But of course... – the mid-twenties weren't yet grown up if they were men.

No sign of Hinnerk; but it was still much too early for the square dancers. But what if they didn't dance today?

"Marga, why don't the square dancers have a fixed date? That should make it difficult scheduling the halls."

"They have two fixed appointments; they just don't take them as a group every time. Often only single couples come for a free practice."

"Why would they do that?"

"This is why." Marga pointed to the door and Madeline turned around.

A firefighter entered the room.

"What...?" Chris – the man Marga had termed a caller. After reading Wikipedia, she knew that they were some kind of instructor for the square dance groups. "What's he doing with the fire department?" He had traces of soot on his face and looked exhausted.

"Medical service. Chris doesn't always get shifts that allow him to train the group. And sometimes he cancels from one minute to the next because he can't get away."

"Because there's a fire somewhere."

Chris noticed Madeline's look and answered with an amused smile. What was he so amused about? A light danced in his brown eyes, giving them golden reflexes.

He came to the counter with his arms at an angle. "Will you please unlock the shower, Marga? I don't want to leave my marks on everything."

Marga picked up the key under the counter.

"I'll handle this." Madeline reached for it. "You have enough to do here."

"You're new! Do you know your way around?"

Madeline opened her mouth for a snarky reply; in that moment, Robert grunted angrily. She nodded, her gaze at Chris. Surely he didn't mean to be unkind.

She awkwardly hoisted herself down from the bar stool. Of course he couldn't help her, but Robert only had to stretch out a hand. Another time, he was constantly groping her.

She was walking down the hallway next to Chris. "Was it bad?" It was just right, if Robert got annoyed she was talking to him.

"The fire?" The light disappeared from his eyes. "A child. But it will live."

"What are you doing? First aid?"

"Too." He pointed to one of the doors. "I'll take that one."

After he disappeared in the shower, she remained for another moment, hesitating. She would have liked to keep talking. Paramedic with the fire brigade during a fire operation; that was surely exciting. So far she had only thought of ambulances and the emergency doctors. He was certainly on ambulance duty, too.

Robert had a new beer in front of him.

"Do you want to drink that now?" She looked at the clock. "We're about to start."

"You weren't here," he hissed.

"How long did you think it would take to unlock a shower?"

She left him and went into the dance hall. Werner Heinemann, the treasurer, was alone that evening and and quite happy to dance with her. But when the first beats were playing, Robert rushed in. Without asking, he pulled her away. Too surprised, also Werner forgot to protest.

"Robert!" Ines' sharp voice drowned out the music.

"I have everything well in hand," he called back just as loudly. Quite true. But this was the last night she danced with him.

As she stepped on his foot for the second time, he stopped. "If you keep this up, you'll never make a good dancer!"

She let him go. "I can't concentrate if you keep blowing your beer breath in my face."

"I for one, want to learn it." A vein on Robert's forehead began to pulsate; he grabbed her more firmly. "Come here!"

"Then find a partner who will live up to your expectations." But she still shouldn't step on his foot on purpose; she didn't want to be considered incompetent now.

Immediately afterwards she was distracted by Hinnerk's laughter, which made its way to them into the hall to them, and she kicked him yet again. The buzz of voices at the bar became louder; then Ines closed the door. Madeline pulled herself together and survived the remainder of the dance circle without any further incidents.

She waited until everyone had left the hall. "Robert, maybe you should find yourself a new partner."

"But Madeline! Your grandfather..."

"... doesn't have to dance with you. I'm tired of you hitting on me. I. Do. Not. Want. It."

Robert stared at her. In his face unbelief changed into disappointment, disappointment into anger. "You could have told me that before."

What would he have gained? She rather did not ask him; she did not need that discussion.

Again Hinnerk's laughter lured her. She craned her neck.

Tanja Walters was standing next to him. Where did she suddenly come from, now that the dance circle was over?

Robert followed her gaze. He studied the girl at length. "Well, then... I guess I won't see you next Friday."

"I'm sorry!" But that wasn't true; she had said it without thinking.

A second woman had now joined Hinnerk and Tanja; much older, perhaps in her late thirties. They were discussing something: according to the movements, some dance steps.

Tanja was just shaking her head vigorously as someone approached her from behind and took her by the shoulders. She turned around laughing and greeted him with a little kiss. Then she came up to Madeline.

"Where did you leave your brother today?" Madeline asked.

Tanja shrugged. "He's caught a major case of flu. That's why I was able to skip the dance circle today. I'm only doing it for Axel's sake anyway."

"Then why are you here now?"

"Therefore." Tanja pointed over to the big hall.

Madeline looked at her perplexed. "Don't tell me you're square dancing too!"

"Sure. It's much more fun!"

"That's what Hinnerk also said."

"What about me? Is there something wrong with me?" Suddenly he stood behind them.

Tanja laughed and leaned against his shoulder. Something like envy pervaded Madeline.

"Tanja is your partner?"

"No." He smirked. "She's found someone better." He pointed to a handsome man whose hair was even blonder than his own.

"You'd be as good as Micky if you danced regularly." Tanja lowered her voice. "And if you had a more talented partner."

Hinnerk shrugged. "There's no other way. And as long as Bettina can stand it with me..."

Chris was marching down the hallway. He had exchanged the uniform for boots in western design, tight-fitting black jeans and a red shirt. His hair was glistening wet from the shower and he wore a cheerful smile on his face. What a man!

His gaze crossed that of Madeline and his smile deepened.

Slowly he came up to the bar, the gaze at her face. "Did you stay for us?" Just how did he figure that?

Before she could deny it, Hinnerk replied. "I suggested Madeline to watch," he said. "Because she doesn't really like ballroom dancing."

"Watch?" Chris grinned. "Better try it straight away."

Tanja creased her forehead. "Although..." She turned around and waved to her partner. "Micky, may I loan you?"

"No way!" He looked around like in search of something. "With whom should I cheat on you?

She linked arms with Madeline. "Madeline is new to the club and not yet committed. We could win her over to our group if you make a good impression."

"Oh, dear." Micky made a sheepish face. "Of all people, you assign such a responsible job to me?"

Madeline listened to the exchange with growing delight. Then she shook her head despite that. "First of all, I'll watch. Though I've read about it, it didn't give me much of an idea." Her gaze went to Chris. "You work with the group differently than other dance instructors?"

"Chris is not an instructor; he's our caller." Micky punched him in the ribs. "Indispensable. Sly."

"Sly?" Madeline's mouth stood open.

"What he sometimes makes up, beggars all description. The real Americans can't do that."

Chris laughed. "Am I not a real American?"

"You don't have to execute yourself what you want us to do."

"Let's start before we have another fire." Chris sent them to the hall. "I'm on call."

Madeline sat on a bar stool to watch.

The dancers formed two squares. Chris looked at her; his grin became challenging as he waved to her. She blushed and quickly turned to Marga.

"I don't have to cram tomorrow. Give me a Prosecco, please."

"What is it with you?"

She grinned. "I'm celebrating the liberation from Robert. I hope he finds the next partner in another club."

"He's not a bad guy, Madeline. Just a little lonely."

"I'm not surprised." When she heard Chris' voice, she took another look into the dance hall. He now spoke English and had a tone that sounded sharp and resolute. "Sounds like Ines to the second power. Does he have to tell them every step?"

Marga laughed. "What kind of a mess do you think it'd be otherwise?" She smirked. "It's a mess anyway."

Chris was commanding. The dancers were walking in circles, the women with the clock, the men counter-clockwise; as they passed by each other they shook hands. Then it became convoluted; they somehow met in the middle of the squares and suddenly everyone had a different place.

"Ring a Ring o' Roses for adults. Are there even tournaments for the square dancers?"

"You can't compare that. They may be more... family reunions. Or some such thing."

Madeline giggled. "So it's typical American." She turned all the way to the hall. Again, her gaze crossed that of Chris and so she simply cheered to him. But instead of helping her overcome her embarrassment, she felt even more intimidated by his intense gaze. Somehow he had little resemblance to the Americans she had seen as a child in Zehlendorf. No hedgehog cut, no gum in his mouth. But perhaps the Americans had changed since they were no longer occupying forces, as Grandma had always called them.

He approached one of the couples and took the man's place. The dancer laughed as she spun into his arm. Even at this distance it was evident that Chris was stiffening as if she had got too close to him during the movement. Would the women in the group be hitting on him? A man looking like this surely didn't miss out on anything.

Then Chris switched on the music; it sounded surprisingly modern. The dancers moved to the rhythm of the music in their positions; he took a microphone in his hand. *"And bow to the partner... join and circle to the left, circle to the right and promenade..."* More and more, the calls were picking up the melody – and then he sang them.

Madeline stared at him with her mouth open. His voice was full and deep and so sexy that it took her breath away.

When her gaze met his again, he laughed. He laughed at her and with a gesture of his hand enticed her to come closer. His laughter reached his eyes and he licked his upper lip; a languid, sensual movement. What were those thoughts just sneaking into her brain? No one had ever looked at her like that before.

He attracted her; she slipped from the barstool and went to the hall door.

Chris sang on; the dancers returned to their original partners and spun them around in a circle. He watched until the movement was over and everyone was back in place.

Then he turned the music down. "I have a new sequel... A partner to demonstrate..." His gaze went from one to the other, then he turned sideways. His eyes sparkled mischievously as he approached Madeline. "Since no one knows this yet, you need not be afraid."

She automatically straightened. "Why should I be afraid?" Yet she took a half step back when he reached out to her. But if she didn't want to make a fool of herself, she had to go with him.

"I just wanted to watch," she whispered in his ear. The smell of his shampoo reached her nose.

Chris stroked the back of her hand with his thumb and her mouth became dry. "It's not difficult," he whispered back.

Madeline concentrated on her feet as he announced the sequence of steps and led her into the movement. His left hand lay on her hip and directed her with gentle pressure. She looked down persistently.

After slowly performing the short sequence twice with her, he turned up the music again and danced the movement with her. Not only did he have more momentum; in the spin he also drew her much closer to him. When he had her in his arms, he held her for a moment.

She would have started fighting Robert a long time ago. Before he even got that close. But this didn't feel like he was imposing himself on her. She looked Chris straight in the eyes. His laughter lines deepened when he noticed. How old could he be?

He bent to her ear. "You're doing fine!"

Madeline laughed nervously. "That would be something, if you'd embarrassed me now."

He nodded. "Then I'd be a bad teacher." He stopped and let go of her to turn to the squares. "Okay?"

He reached for the microphone; then he glanced to Madeline with a frown. "Tanja, will you leave your partner to Madeline for ten minutes?"

Tanja laughed. "I anticipated that." She stepped out of her square and walked towards Madeline. "Don't be a coward."

Madeline raised her head. "I said right away..."

Tanja interrupted her with a smile. "Cling together, swing together!"

Chris frowned suspiciously. "What does that mean?"

"An old saying. From the Stone Age or something." Madeline raised her chin even higher and took the place next to Micky. "At least, you won't risk any kicking if you accept this swap."

"That clearly speaks in favor of square dancing; don't you think?" Micky linked arms with her and Chris started with the calls. To Madeline's horror, however, he did not begin with what she had just practiced with him. She hesitated, but Micky pushed her into the direction she was supposed to go.

Again her gaze met Chris. He looked at her provokingly. She certainly wouldn't chicken out; what was he thinking?

Shortly afterwards he whispered with Tanja, his gaze constantly directed at Madeline. Tanja's stare became more and more mischievous.

"You're not getting out of here any more, Madeline." Micky now also smirked. "Tanja's cooking up something." He exchanged a conspiratorial look with Hinnerk when the two men shook hands afterwards. When Madeline squinted to the clock above the bar, it had been far more than ten minutes that she now followed Micky. It didn't feel like that. Time had flown by in a flash.

Chris started to play a faster piece. Then he stopped the CD and approached her. "Do you like to continue until the end of the practice?"

Now she was surprised that he even asked her. She was

looking for a sign from Tanja and as the girl nodded to her, she agreed. Hinnerk played a pantomime of applause; of course. She laughed boisterously before she asked Micky to explain what he expected from her right now.

This dance had many fast spins and her square reached a new peak of silliness and laughter. Chris stood in front of the stereo grinning and singing the calls.

Madeline beamed at her dance partner; then she beamed at Hinnerk and finally also at Chris. Incredible that Grandpa had such a group in his club. It wasn't like him at all.

After practice everyone was standing at the bar and Marga put two bottles of Prosecco, a red Beaujolais Primeur and a white Edelzwicker on the counter.

"My turn," said a man who had to be about Chris' age. He reached out to Madeline. "I'm Norbert Kaminski. Are you joining us now?"

"Well." Heat spread on Madeline's face. "I'm in the dance circle and I was just curious. I'd rather stop dancing altogether."

Chris looked over to them. "Why would you do that?"

"No time." Madeline raised her shoulders. "I need A levels for university admission."

Norbert smiled. "It's not healthy to spend all day at school or at a desk. You know, '*Mens sana...*'"

Madeline giggled. "Now you're exposed. You're a teacher!"

The roaring laughter of the bystanders and the flaming blush in Norbert's face confirmed that she had hit the mark.

Hinnerk approached Madeline from behind and handed her a Prosecco. "Saw you drink that tickling water all the time." He gave his second glass, a red wine, to Norbert, who frowned at that.

"I was faster." Hinnerk grinned at him.

"That was my rounds today." Norbert looked even gloomier.

Hinnerk slapped him on the back. "Come on! Better keep your money together or you'll get in trouble with your ex again."

"Do you want to discuss which one of you is more broke?" Tanja took a hefty sip of her Edelzwicker. "You can't compete with me anyway."

"Then we should buy you an extra one." The elaborately coiffed girl, who had danced with Norbert, punched Tanja into the side. "Or I could give you some of my tips."

Despite her overdone hairstyle, Madeleine immediately liked the girl. Suddenly she realized how many of the group she liked at first sight. "Do you work in a restaurant?"

The girl squeezed her lips together; for a moment she looked quite grumpy. "No!" That grumpy face again. "I'm learning hairdressing."

"Oh, that's why you have such a great coiffure!"

"But that's the only thing Carola gets out of this apprenticeship!" Norbert's face reflected Carola's thoughts.

"Then why are you learning it?" Madeline blushed at the question; hopefully this wasn't too intrusive. But Carola just shrugged. Okay, no topic for here.

Carola turned to Chris and immediately the grumpiness disappeared from her posture and face. Her eyes flashed merrily as she spoke to him. She certainly had a crush on him.

Madeline started chewing nervously on her lower lip. Just why did it bother her? She met Marga's watchful gaze and blushed again. Hastily she put her half-full glass on the counter. "I'm afraid I have to go home. Cramming!" She waved both hands to say goodbye to everyone at the same time.

As she had put on her coat and walked to the door, Hinnerk came after her. "Will you come again next time?"

She looked back. "I don't know." Chris had one hand on Carola's arm. "No, I guess not; I have to cram for my written exams."

Hinnerk nodded. "That's more important than dancing, of course."

"But?" Madeline smirked instinctively. "Such a sentence is always followed by a 'but'."

"I have no argument you haven't heard already."

Chris had taken out his cell and read a text with his brows raised. She opened the door and strolled down the stairs.

As she entered the yard, Chris stormed past her. Was there another fire somewhere? Tiled stoves were still used for heating in the old building quarters...

5

At noon on Tuesday a message from Hinnerk flashed in Madeline's inbox. Where did he get her e-mail address? Bettina had caught the flu and now he wanted her as a replacement. "If for once I have time to dance," he closed his mail, "then you won't want me to stand by and watch." Surely Marga had had her hand in this.

Madeline closed the mails, unwrapped some chocolate and devoted herself to her homework: an essay about the seriousness of Hollande in delivering on his campaign promises. *"Il n'a pas les moyens"*, she started with verve. Then she pushed the keyboard away. How could she now justify that it wasn't his fault, though he had all the power?

She thoughtfully nibbled the chocolate. Then she reopened her mail app. Until she could think of something, she could answer Hinnerk. He was too nice to pretend she hadn't seen his mail in time. In fact, he was too nice to condemn him to just watch.

She looked at her watch and did the math. If she could get done half of the essay by five, she could write the rest after the square dance.

"Hi Hinnerk, I'm sitting over my homework. If you can quickly give me three reasons why Hollande will involuntarily break his campaign promises, I'll come to square dance tonight." She sent the mail and went downstairs to fetch a bottle of grape juice.

When she came back to her room, the mail butler was displayed on the screen. Hinnerk had delivered what she needed. Mind-boggling. Perhaps geologists had to be familiar also with the politics of the countries in which they worked.

Now she had no choice but to fulfill her part of the deal. In fact, she was looking forward to it. "You're a darling," she mailed back. "See you in a few."

Shortly before five she had written her essay completely; in any case she only had to polish a little. She had never been this fast before. As if the momentum of dancing reached all the way to her desk.

One minute before the start of the practice she ran up the stairs to the club rooms. The square dancers were already in the hall, including Hinnerk. He had counted on her to keep her word. He trusted her; that was a good feeling.

"I finished writing that thing," she shouted as she peeled herself out of her coat.

He came towards her, laughing. "And you're on time, too!"

She let him take her by the hand and lead her to her position. "Thanks to your help. Your cues were brilliant."

"I'm glad you came, Madeline." Chris' warm voice let a shiver run down her back.

His gaze drove the next shiver down her spine. She quickly looked away, but she knew he wouldn't let her out of his sight. She was the total beginner here, so he watched out for her. But a voice in her head told her that this was not the reason.

After announcing the calls he would start with, he approached Madeline. "Have you got that?"

"I hope so."

With a hand movement he engaged Hinnerk and he led

Madeline through the steps, while Chris repeated the calls. In the end, he nodded. "You did good, Madeline." He stepped back. "And now everybody." He started the music.

Often Madeline was one step behind because she did not understand quickly enough what she should be doing. But it didn't seem to spoil anyone's mood; Hinnerk's least of all. Every time she was separated from him, he shouted overly detailed instructions to her. Soon the others did the same and within ten minutes their square became a goofy bunch of jesters.

Then, in the middle of a piece Chris switched off the music. Shocked, Madeline turned to him. Oh, that couldn't have gone well.

He laughed at her. Surprised, she gasped. In every other group of the club there would have been a sermon by the coach now; she was sure of that.

"Difficult, Madeline?" Why did he call her by her name in every sentence?

She stepped uncomfortably from one foot to the other. "Things are so different."

"Sure. But you were good. We'll do it again, though."

Madeline felt like flying while she kept dancing. And she only rarely made a mistake. Meanwhile she also got used to Chris' American English; actually it was even easier to understand than the British she learned at school.

"One time slowly and without music." This was not a repetition, but a different succession of calls, in some way obviously also unusual for the others. Chris let them stop and repeat several times.

"I thought you could all do it," Madeline whispered in Tanja's ear when they crossed once.

"The tricky thing is the order of the calls. Chris constantly thinks of something different."

At the next encounter with Tanja Madeline asked: "And that works? New every time? This is totally different compared to the Latin formation."

"That's why it's so much more entertaining here." Tanja exuberantly whirled Madeline back into Hinnerk's arms.

"Mistake, Tanja," Chris shouted.

Tanja stopped. "That was on purpose."

Chris raised his index finger, grinning. "Do you have to put on a show like this every time we have a newcomer in the group?"

"As if it happens that often."

"Sure." Chris' gaze was stuck on Madeline again. "Five minutes break and then the whole sequence with music." He repeated the order of the calls. "Memorize it."

Tanja made a face. "You're a martinet, Chris."

He shrugged, amused, and looked for another piece of music. Madeline was once again surprised at the tone in the group. Nobody seemed to take the whole thing seriously and yet they were good. The second square was actually very good. And she was sure that hers would be, too, if they didn't have to struggle with her.

She vowed to herself to do everything right on the next repetition. Quietly she tried to repeat the sequence of the calls. Hinnerk listened and helped her when she got stuck. Chris watched them, but he didn't interfere.

"Do you have got the sequence in your head?" Chris asked Hinnerk after the break. Since he nodded, he sent him to the mike and took Madeline by her hand.

They switched places? Madeline panicked. When Chris put his arm around her waist, her hands got wet with agitation.

Chris' mouth was close to her ear. "Don't worry; I won't bite." He made a throaty sound. "Not now."

"Sometimes you do, then," she dared to say.

"On special occasions." What she read in his eyes undoubtedly spoke of one specific occasion. To what kind of thoughts took her this man? He was way too old for her. She certainly didn't have a father complex; no girl could wish for a better one than Bruno was.

"Madeline?" His voice caressed her, "You weren't paying attention." No rebuke, just an observation.

She nevertheless brought out her apology with a stutter. "I'm a little nervous today." – "You make me nervous," she should have said to be honest.

Chris increased the pressure of his hand on her hip; it felt good. "Did I already say that I don't bite? You can trust me."

Madeline stopped breathing a second time. She knew exactly what he meant. And she believed him.

The remainder of the evening she tried to concentrate on dancing. After Hinnerk was her partner again, she avoided looking in Chris' direction. But she felt it every time when his gaze was on her. He is too old for you, she said to herself incessantly, and strove to intensify contact with Hinnerk. But when he reacted to it, she was ashamed. It wasn't right to flirt with him if he didn't see it as a pastime, too. And about that she wasn't sure at all.

Then the practice was finished and Tanja put her arm around Madeline's shoulder. "It's much nicer here than in the dance circle; don't you think?"

She really couldn't deny that now.

Hinnerk beamed expectantly. "So you're in?"

No, she certainly couldn't do that. She had to avoid Chris and in Hinnerk she shouldn't raise false hopes. "I can't; I don't have a partner. Anyway, you're rather lacking a man because of Hinnerk's travels."

"That doesn't have to stop you, Madeline." Chris' habit of always saying her name made her increasingly nervous. He came closer and she would have liked to take to her heels when he looked right into her eyes. "Some dancer would be happy if she could miss a performance for once in a while without messing things up."

"At the moment everyone feels obliged to come to every practice if she's not actually crawling on all fours." Carola handed her a glass of Prosecco.

"And I don't make organization easy with these constantly changing practice schedules." Chris looked at her pleadingly. She suspected that it wasn't for the group's sake that he wanted her to return.

Her answer came automatically. "I have to cram. Actually, I don't have any time to dance."

Tanja growled. "You don't make me believe that. I was at the *Collège Français*, too." She laughed at Madeline's baffled look. "And you had time for the dance circle, as well."

Madeline was getting hotter and hotter as she searched for another excuse. But Chris's wait-and-see look made it impossible to think. "I'd have to learn all your moves first. It's all that different from ballroom dancing." Chris' gaze became even more intense; she knew exactly what he was thinking. "I... I'll talk to my parents." Certainly he now considered her a chicken.

Chris' gaze blatantly showed his unbelief. "Don't you yourself know best how much time you need to study?" Unexpectedly a warm smile spread on his face; did he know again what was on her mind? "We don't want to talk you into it. It wouldn't do anyone any good."

"I'll call."

Chris reached into his pocket and gave her a card. He actually had business cards. Bewildered, she gasped and quickly put the card in her pocket. Better she went home now.

In her haste, she didn't even say goodbye to Marga. Chris' gaze was burning in her back.

Chris' card had an e-mail address and three phone numbers: Mobile, home and work. The private phone number was a Schmargendorf number – or would have been in the old days, but now people could take their phone number with them when they moved across Berlin. Madeline gave in to temptation and looked for him in the phone book. He actually lived almost around the corner. If she didn't board at the nearest bus stop on the way to school and continued walking a bit... His sparkling gaze pursued her into her sleep.

Before she headed to school the next morning, she turned on the computer and sent him a mail: "I'm in. M."

When she came home in the late afternoon, a whole army of smileys flashed at her in reply. "Awesome!"

Disappointing; she had expected a few more words. After all, he had to thank her. Then she noticed that he had sent the answer just minutes after her message – maybe he had to go to work?

Shouldn't she call now to ask if the next practice session would be on Friday or not until Tuesday?

While she was skulking around the phone, Konstanze called her into the kitchen. Madeline took the chopping board and the leek. Konstanze ran the potatoes through the food processor to cut them into slices for a *gratin dauphinois*.

"Visitors? Grandpa and Grandma are coming for dinner?"

Konstance's face got a downright sly expression. "Since when is this the only visit that calls on us?"

"So who's coming?"

Konstanze must have noticed her relief. She sat across from Madeline. "What do you have going on with your grandfather? Is this about dancing?" Sometimes Madeline suspected

that she was quite pleased when she messed with Grandpa —
as if she didn't dare do it herself.

"If you would like to tell me something, child; I am listening to you."

"It's nothing much." Madeline cut the roots off the leeks.
"Grandpa already knows that I have no desire to learn to
dance the way he imagines. Nor that I have the time now."
She began to remove the dried out tips and outer layers.

"But yesterday you did go dancing."

Maman could really be pushy; and nonetheless she acted
so innocent. "Not really. I was just..." She shrugged. "I was
just doing a favor for someone who helped me with my
homework."

Konstanze showed her flatly that she didn't believe a word.
"That's why I had finished early." She shrugged again. "Just
for entertainment."

Konstanze's gaze became increasingly thoughtful. Nevertheless, Madeline stuck to her cover-up tactics. "It's important
to clear your head from time to time."

Konstanze laughed out loud. "There's more to it than that,
am I right?" She patted her arm. "Watch your back, Madeline.
You're still so young."

At that she'd rather not protest; that was clearly an offer
of alliance. "If I have a problem, I'll tell you."

Now Konstanze appeared to want to ask something anyway, but then she turned around and continued to devote
herself to the *gratin*. Grandpa should only dare to question
her decision — with Konstanze at her side he wouldn't achieve
anything.

6

Chris had sent Madeline a mail inviting her to come half an hour earlier to practice. With trembling fingers she typed her assent.

When she arrived, he was sitting at the bar with a glass of mineral water. Mineral water! She was impressed.

"We're good to go." Wordlessly, he went ahead of her into the hall and turned on the music. "For the atmosphere." He smiled for the first time. "It sets you into rhythm more easily."

As he grabbed her arm, she winced. His eyes widened in surprise and he let her go. She reached for his hand; he should not think she had recoiled from him.

He stared at her as if to read her mind. Then he cleared his throat and muttered something in English before explaining the first call.

But instead of looking at his movements, she looked at his face the whole time.

"Let's try; will you?" He drew her closer to him and Madeline was overwhelmed by the same feeling that had already paralyzed her brain the week before.

She unintentionally pressed in closer to him and shut her eyes halfway while she let him guide her. Then came a moment when his breath caressed her cheek. If she turned her head now, they would touch. Should she? She swallowed nervously; what would he think of her?

"Madeline?" Also his voice caressed her. "Did you just listen to me?"

She opened her eyes completely. "I'm sorry. I'm going to focus."

His gaze was watchful, a little suspicious. "Is everything all right?"

Nothing was all right. "Yes, of course. I've been sitting on my exam preparations too long. I'd need to sleep in for once."

The suspicion did not vanish from his gaze, but he smiled. "If I can arrange it, we'll use Tuesday for practice; so you can get to bed early. Your *Abitur* must not fail because of us."

"It won't." She exhaled; that was more familiar ground. "However, I need a straight A-levels for my place at university."

"What are you gonna study?"

"Medicine."

"Oh!" His gaze showed surprise. "Then we have a common interest. However, I was defeated by the lack of a scholarship. Alas, Dad being in the Air Force didn't help me enough."

"And that's why you're with the fire department now?"

He nodded. And cleared his throat again. "Now we both haven't been focusing. We're not finished yet."

Nor did they finish, because Hinnerk came right afterwards. They couldn't refuse his offer to practice with Madeline.

All of a sudden Madeline felt clumsy and stiff. Chris' gaze seemed to express disapproval. She stopped. "What am I doing wrong?"

"Huh?" Hinnerk looked at her in astonishment. "Nothing. Why would you think that?"

Chris said nothing at all; he repeated his last call and Hinnerk started anew.

On this evening Chris surprised the square dancers with calls that were obviously so unusual in their order that they created confusion more than once. He was more exuberant than usual; Madeline no longer saw anything of disapproval.

His high spirits got Madeline sassy. She intentionally mis-danced because she hoped he would take matters into his own hands and personally show her how it was done. But the Tuesday before had probably been an exception to facilitate her start. Instead, he first let her change partners, then her square had to pause completely so she could watch the other one.

After that, she preferred to do everything correctly. She didn't want to screw up with her square. Once she met Chris' watchful gaze: Had he seen through her? She decided to enjoy the evening and leave everything else to time.

After practice Chris was gone, as soon as he had said goodbye to them.

When she got home, she sent him a mail asking if he would practice with her again beforehand. "After it," Chris wrote back. He was on duty before.

7

Square dancing was actually quite simple once you knew what was behind such strange calls as "pass the ocean" or "weave the ring". Hinnerk nodded approvingly over and over again. Madeline enjoyed the atmosphere in the group, the music – and the beguiling sound of Chris' singing voice. Every time she looked at him, she felt like she had his undivided attention.

If she told Grandpa that after the flop with Robert she had simply seized the next opportunity offered to her? Actually, that should please him. Dancing was dancing... No, it wasn't. Exactly why she would stick to square dancing. Her throat tightened at the thought of Chris.

Madeline was so immersed in brooding that she began to make mistakes. Chris' critically furrowed forehead told her to better pull herself together. He shouldn't think she was doing it on purpose again.

Then practice was over and the group gathered at the bar as usual. Chris stood with the others and chatted; had he decided she didn't need extra tuition?

Monopolized by Hinnerk, Madeline sipped indecisively on her Prosecco. Soon it was obvious that he would have liked to ask what was wrong with her. But to her relief, he didn't do it after all.

Then Carola and Tanja wanted to leave and Norbert asked Madeline if he should take her along.

Chris noticed Madeline at a loss and came to them. Obviously he had looked after her the whole time, although he had appeared absorbed in the conversations. "It's late; but do you still have time to stay?"

"Yes, of course." Like she hadn't been waiting for this all along.

Hinnerk's gaze became even more watchful. "Practice? I can stay too."

Chris' face remained blank when he replied. "That's not necessary." Why didn't he explicitly send Hinnerk away?

But Hinnerk didn't seem to suspect anything and when Chris went back into the hall with her, he just stood in the doorway for a moment and said goodbye before they even started dancing.

Madeline was tense with excitement and when Chris took her by the hand, she felt like being covered in a treacherous blush. To hide what was going on in her, she tensed up even more. But it didn't help.

Chris held her on both shoulders and studied her face. "Easy, Madeline." He smiled sparingly; his gaze sent goose bumps down her back.

She leaned into him and he fiercely sucked in the air. He smelled of peppermint and a tart aftershave, although it must have been hours ago that he had shaved. The dark shadow on his cheeks gave him an audacious expression.

She couldn't think of an answer that was somehow funny or intelligent. But she began to relax. And the whole time she had the feeling he had to make an effort to stay cool. There was nothing left of the easiness of the last days. At some point she gave up thinking about it and just danced.

"I'll take you home," he said when at the bar the glasses were clinking with Marga's cleaning up. Obviously, that was the sign to end it. Did Marga actually wait until the last one left in the evening? But Chris certainly had a key to the floor.

Then the three of them left together, but Marga rejected Chris' offer to take her home as well. "I need fresh air and exercise before I can sleep."

It had started snowing again and the snow stood out brightly against the unlit courtyard. "The janitor is probably back in the pub," Marga grumbled as she followed them stepping in their footsteps with her arms slightly outstretched.

Chris took Madeline by the hand to guide her safely over the slippery surface.

Marga stopped at the street. "We'll get home faster if we don't ride with you, Chris. Until you have dug out your car and then with the slippery roads..." She looked at Madeline invitingly. But as she didn't react, Marga said goodbye and trudged to the subway station.

Chris' car was only a few steps away, but when Madeline got in, she already had icy feet and hands. It must have been fifteen degrees below zero. She squeezed her hands under her armpits while Chris cleared the windows all around. Before he drove off, he reached for a thermal blanket in the back seat and wrapped Madeline in it.

"You exaggerate!"

He grinned. "Once learnt, never forgotten."

She took a closer look at the blanket. "Is that perhaps one from the fire department?"

"It's one like those we use with the fire department." Chris pressed the start button and after a moment of reflection the combustion engine started.

Winter road maintenance vehicles were only occasionally on the move and Chris preferred the main roads to the city ring freeway. After the battery got warm, they rolled silently through the snow-covered city. It was slippery and again and again the Toyota braked by itself, because the wheels started to slide.

Marga had been right; she certainly got home faster by subway. But Madeline had to change several times for the way home and she would have frozen her feet at the bus stops,

Chris was taciturn. From time to time, he gave her a look out of the corner of his eye that she did not know how to read. She was directing him and that was all she said.

The tension between them grew.

"Thank you," she muttered as he stopped at her door.

"It's been a pleasure."

She came to meet him unintentionally as he turned to her.

He gave her a fleeting kiss on the cheek.

Madeline's breath faltered; then she turned her head and her lips met. His mouth was warm and soft and opened under her touch. She deepened the kiss and he answered with his tongue. But then he withdraw.

"Madeline." He cleared his throat. "We can't do this."

She snorted outragedly. "I'm almost eighteen!"

"Almost!" He closed his eyes for a moment, then reached for her and pulled her to him.

To get even closer, she wrapped her arms around his neck. "Kiss me, Chris." She rubbed her face against his cheek; he moaned. "Kiss me, Chris." She slowly stroked his lips with two fingers.

He made a noise that sounded like a dog growling from the bottom of its throat. "You're driving me crazy, Madeline." He pulled her in his lap. And then he kissed her; intense, demanding, until she was out of breath. Her insides ignited.

With her eyes closed, she lay in his arm and tracked the hot waves rolling through her body. What a dizzying feeling. That a simple kiss could have such an effect... but it hadn't been just a simple kiss. Chris was crazy about her, there was no doubt.

"Chris..."

He put one hand on her mouth, stroking her cheek with his thumb. "It's time you get home."

"All is dark here; no one can see us. And my parents are at the *Friedrichstadtpalast*." She slipped back into her seat. "Would you like to see my butterfly collection?"

"What?" He looked at her as if she had lost her mind.

"That was a running gag. I would never impale the beautiful butterflies."

The laughter lines around his eyes deepened and were now visible even in the twilight of the street. "Sleep tight, Madeline."

"I'll dream of you, Chris."

His gaze was pure, undisguised tenderness. She got out of the car in a buoyant mood and trudged across the driveway to the front door.

When she turned around, he had silently driven away. Madeline smiled. In less than two months she'd turn eighteen.

She got a glass of milk and then turned on her computer. "Good night," Chris had written her from his cell. He was most certainly in love with her.

8

"Hello Marga! Let someone on the board say once again that young people are not interested in our old dance." Chris put the bag with his uniform on her desk. "You can add a new dancer to the square dance." He beamed.

Marga changed the program and called up the members' file. "Who do you mean as the new dancer? Madeline? George certainly won't be happy about that."

"Why? Because she gets lost to the dance circle? Not because of us!"

"George already saw his granddaughter as a new star in the tournament sky…"

Chris stared at her with his mouth open. What did she just say?

"What's the matter?"

He took a breath. "Why granddaughter?"

"Who did you think Madeline Lagrange would be?"

"Until now, I didn't know her last name." He rubbed his face with a tired gesture. "This indeed…" Not enough that Madeline was only seventeen; she was also the chairman's granddaughter.

It couldn't have been more complicated.

"What should happen?" Marga copied Madeline's data into the table of the square dance group. "I'll send her phone number and e-mail address to your cell."

"I already have the mail." He pulled the cell out of his

pocket and leafed through the calendar, announcing the next practice dates to Marga. "I was able to convince my colleagues that I need to plan longer ahead. Unless there are crises, the shift schedule is set for the next four weeks."

"What did you trade it for with them?"

He shrugged. "I have no family; I can do the inconvenient shifts without hurting anyone."

"Very selfless!" Marga winked.

What was with her? He frowned; mockery wasn't like Marga. Was it because of that extra lesson with Madeline? "There's always a price to pay." He took his CDs out of the office cabinet and went to the big hall to pick the tunes he wanted to use that night.

Now he had Madeline registered as a group member. But would she even come after that kiss? She had not reacted to his bedtime greeting.

"A water, Chris?" Marga came out of the office with a crate of beverages and began to put them into the fridge at the bar.

He had preferred to have a beer now. Or even a whiskey. But that was not compatible with his job; and he would then smell of alcohol.

He opened his mineral water and went through the first CD. "Pickin' up Strangers" – the first piece where he'd held Madeline in his arms. The memory alone was enough to arouse his desire. He should never have danced with her. After all, he was the smarter one, the adult; twice as old as Madeline.

Too old.

The slamming of the hall door shook him from his thoughts.

Madeline threw herself into his arms and kissed him impetuously. He couldn't help but answer her kiss. He sank into her warmth, into the delicate scent of her hair. Her warmth spread within him and it only took seconds until he reacted fervently.

He turned his head to the side. "Madeline…" Apparently all he could think of in her presence was to say her strange name over and over again.

"I purposely closed the door." She kissed him on the cheek, stroked his chin with her mouth and then had her lips on his again.

He moaned. "Stop that!"

Madeline flinched, her eyes shimmering wet. "Don't you like me?" She sounded so pitiful that he pressed her against him anew.

"Dearest, wonderful Madeline." He brushed a curl from her forehead before releasing her again and taking half a step back. "You're underage and on top of that, I'm your coach!"

Defiance and anger were painted on her face. "That doesn't interest me. I won't be ordered around!" She'd be stamping her foot in a minute.

Chris reached out to her. "Come here!"

Her eyes shot off lightnings; now her wrath was on him. "And I won't let you order me around either." She burst out laughing. "Oh, obviously I have to." And another thunderstorm in her face. "But not like this!"

Her fickle temper was intoxicating. "What's the harm if we stand down until you're of age?" He waited almost eagerly for the feelings that would now appear on her face.

Pout. She sat next to him on the edge of the table. "We're not living in the Middle Ages. Nobody cares."

"Conversely, it gets right. In the Middle Ages, the age of girls didn't matter."

Madeline began to knead her earlobe; but before she opened her mouth again, the hall door was opened.

She turned around in shock; this way she didn't see him exhale in relief.

Norbert and Carola stood in the doorway; Norbert with a furrowed brow as if he suspected something. "If you keep practicing so often, Madeline will soon be rivaling us all."

"Didn't the ladies want the opportunity to excuse themselves without a guilty conscience?" That was probably not very convincing; but what else could he say?

"We haven't been practicing." Madeline in her thoughtlessness!

The frown lines on Norbert's brow became deeper. He needed an opportunity to talk to him. But that would mean letting Madeline drive home alone.

During the practice Madeline sought him so obviously that soon Hinnerk also frowned. And then Tanja.

Chris couldn't do a thing. If he said anything, the situation actually became suspect. Didn't they know him well enough to trust him? He didn't get a chance to talk to them. After practice Madeline waited as if it were a given until he himself left.

Hinnerk and Norbert had both offered Madeline to ride with them. And both had reacted more than bewildered when she refused and made no preparations to go home already. It was so obvious she was waiting for something – for someone.

Again they left together with Marga, who closed the club behind them. On the street Marga linked arms with him. "Today I accept your offer with pleasure. I want to see my sister."

He forced out a smile. "And the car's not snowed in." The logical course of action was that he first dropped off Madeline. Marga knew that; she knew Madeline's address.

But Madeline didn't know and cheerfully slipped into the passenger seat. She folded down her sun visor and silently watched Marga in the make-up mirror while Marga and Chris were chatting.

When they were near the neighborhood of Schmargendorf, confusion spread on Madeline's face. "Marga, I thought you live in Wilmersdorf."

"But that's not my destination yet." Marga smiled at her innocently in the mirror. So Marga had also become suspicious; he had guessed it. Madeline had made no effort and he had always been a bad actor.

He stopped in front of Madeline's house and her face darkened entirely; her gaze stabbed him. Why did she take her anger out on him and not on Marga, who had smuggled herself into his car without being invited?

When Madeline got out of his car with her chin rebelliously raised not saying goodbye, he was struck with regret. How much he wished now to sink into her kiss...

He looked after her until she disappeared in the house. She hadn't even turned around to him at the door. She was hurt; that he had not wanted. Marga certainly didn't want that either. He drove off with a sigh.

Marga bent to the front in-between the seats. "You don't do anything stupid, do you?"

He preferred not to say anything to that.

"The girl has a crush on you; a blind man can see that. But what about you, Chris?"

"I'm serious about it." He sighed again. "And it makes me sick that she's way too young to properly assess her own feelings." When he turned at the next corner, he took a look at Marga. "I wish she meant it."

"I have never seen you like this, Chris." Now there was a reprimand in Marga's voice. "And she's way too young for you."

"Who can tell." He pressed his lips together.

"Chris!" That was real indignation. "You're old enough to know this is childish. You know each other — for how long? Ten days?"

"Two weeks." His heart was on fire. "But it does exist. Love at first sight."

"Nonsense!" Marga hit the back of his seat with her fist. "You're flattered because a young girl is chasing after you all goggle-eyed. Is this already the midlife crisis for you? You stay out of her way; nothing good can come of it."

Now he was actually alerted. "What do you mean?"

"If George finds out... You're endangering the whole group."

He burst out laughing. "You mean he'll sack me? Square dancing is a thorn in his side anyway."

"All the more reason for you not to give him a cause." She seemed to be really worried. "And you would no longer see the girl either."

"Madeline will be eighteen soon." Now he already used the same rationale as she did. But Marga was right, of course; if George set his sights on it, he would prevail on the board... Even if the group left the club together with him; nothing of it would be good.

But this problem would also arise if Madeline was eighteen. If the chairman did not tolerate a relationship between them, he would have many means to bully him. So far he probably hadn't even realized that Madeline preferred square dancing to the dance circle.

"I'm not saying anything. I'm just saying, you should use your head to think and not..."

"We didn't sleep together! What do you take me for?"

Marga's face told him clearly. But she believed him; she wouldn't tell the board anything.

9

When Madeline entered the kitchen with her shoulders slumped, Konstanze silently poured a peppermint tea, stirred sugar into it and put the cup in front of her.

"Like I'm sick!"

"Sick or not. You look like you could use a little pampering."

Madeline blew cautiously into the cup. "And of course you want to know what's going on."

"Anyway, you should tell somebody."

Madeline placed her elbows on the table and took the cup in both hands. "What for? It doesn't change anything."

"Wow, there's someone who mightily stepped on your toes." Konstanze laughed. "Presumably not in the actual sense of the word..."

Madeline gingerly drank half a cup before reaching for the sugar tongs and letting another piece splash in.

"Who is it?"

Madeline wasn't yet about to confide in her. She fluttered her eyelashes innocently.

"I've never seen you like this, child. It looks like the first real heartache."

"Heartache!" Madeline snorted outragedly. "That's something for teenagers."

"And you ain't one of them no more?"

"In six weeks' time you can't interfere with us any more. Just dare it!"

"Us!" Konstanze put her hands on Madeline's back and turned her towards her. "So, who is it?"

"Chris!" Madeline's eyes filled with tears. "The caller."

"The what?"

"But, *Maman*! The one who leads the square dance group."

Konstanze hugged her. "Is he serious?"

"What do I know!" Madeline snorted. "I have seen how he reacts to me. But I don't know what to make of it."

"Did he tell you he loved you?"

"No. But... but you can feel it nonetheless." A sob tightened her throat. She hadn't dignified him not even with a single word, when she got out of his car. Why had she been so nasty to him?

"Then why are you crying?"

Madeline put the cup down and rested her head in her hands. "This is all so difficult."

"How long have you known him? Really, I mean. You've only been in the group a few weeks."

"That's not what matters." Madeleine's eyes began to glint. "The first time I saw him... We looked at each other across the room and I thought my heart would stop. All of a sudden the air seemed to burn and... and..." She had no words for what she had felt at that moment.

"Love at first sight, you mean?" Konstanze smiled leniently. "Expect to see more often that the sight of a man brings all your senses to life. That's not love, that's sexual attraction. Chemistry. You can't build a life on that."

"What relationship lasts a lifetime? Like you should count on it."

"Well." Konstanze wiggled her index finger half threateningly. "Haven't you learned anything from us? And from Bruno's parents?"

"You and Bruno are the exception that confirms the rule. But Grandpa doesn't really love Friederike for quite some time now. Since she can't dance anymore..." As if the terrible accident had been her fault.

Konstanze took her in her arms and wiped the tears from her face with the back of her hand. "Do you mind if I drive you to the next practice session?"

"What?" Madeline stared at her uncomprehending. "Why would you do that?"

"Hm." Konstanze smiled mischievously. "Now that you've decided to make something permanent with the dancing, I care what kind of people they are."

"You're spying on me?" Madeline clenched her fists and tried to suppress the rising anger.

"If I wanted to spy, I wouldn't tell you anything."

Suspiciously, she squinted her eyes. "You want to know who Chris is."

"Are you surprised? You never talked like that about any of the kids you had a crush on."

"Chris is not a kid!"

Konstanze laughed heartily. "Exactly, that's why."

10

The following Tuesday Chris once again had no time to shower at the station between mission and practice; wet hair would be highly unhealthy in the icy temperatures. Shortly before the start of the practice he entered the club rooms wrapped in his uniform and the smell of smoke.

George was sitting at his desk in the office looking through the mail. On a Tuesday. He turned to him and scrutinized him with a disapproving expression.

"Good evening, George." Chris tried to ignore the premonition of coming disaster. Should he ask him why he had come?

Marga put on a cheery smile. "Have you saved another one, Chris?"

For a moment the disapproval vanished from George's face. "I see it's not easy to reconcile your profession with the work you do here."

"I can manage. In a moment no one would even see what I'm doing with the rest of my life." Chris grinned and raised a sleeve to his nose. "And won't smell it either."

He took his clothes bag out of the closet, grabbed the key to the shower from the wall and left the office whistling.

George's gaze pierced his back. What was that man up to?

When he got out of the shower, the first dancers stood at the bar and George in the office had turned his chair so far to the side that he had them in his field of vision. Like a spider lurking in its web. Even when Madeline came, he kept sitting there.

Madeline greeted everyone with kisses. When she got to Chris, she put her hands on his shoulders. She smelled of cinnamon and something sweet, chocolate maybe.

Her touch electrified him; he quickly pushed her away. "Your grandfather is here."

"My who?" She looked at him in shock. "Grandpa?"

"Did you think I wouldn't know?"

"It's easy. Typical Huguenot surname." Madeline raised her chin. "Everybody here knows that."

He turned away. "Let's start, guys!"

Chris had trouble concentrating. The thought of George's disapproving look would not leave him. After a while George came and stood in the doorway of the hall. Strangely enough, that helped him. It was like a challenge: that he knew how to answer.

From the squares, glances went back and forth between him and George. They had noticed that there was a conflict in the air. The atmosphere was charging. Despite the growing tension, no one made another mistake that evening; also the group had embraced the challenge.

Relieved, Chris finally turned off the stereo.

George was still standing in the doorway, making himself even larger. "You guys are really good." His gaze clung to Madeline. "It's a shame you're wasting your talent on this Ring o' Roses."

Madeline picked up on the provocation before anyone else could react. "Grandpa, the most important thing is that we enjoy it."

She got some bemused looks; so others hadn't known either that she was his granddaughter.

Norbert was panting audibly before he opened his mouth. "George, we appreciate very much that we can dance in this great club nonetheless."

"I'll take you home, Madeline." George finally stepped aside so the square dancers could leave the hall. He took Madeline by the hand.

Her gaze flew to Chris. Before George turned to him, he shook his head. It certainly wouldn't be a good idea to stay for practice now. The old man didn't like the whole thing at all. And he was known for his doggedness.

Maybe it wasn't a good idea anyway to remain alone with Madeline. This challenge he might not be up to. That girl got under his skin like none before.

Marga was deliberately busy putting the usual drinks on the counter.

"George is up to something." Norbert downed his beer in one go and then chucked the can into the litter basket behind the counter. "I didn't know she's his granddaughter."

Hinnerk looked thoughtfully into his glass. "Maybe it was a mistake that I lured her out of the dance circle to come here." His gaze pierced Chris. "Could I have had any idea what the consequences would be?"

A gloomy feeling crept up in Chris that he didn't mean George. But now things were as they were.

When eventually all the square dancers were gone, he went to the office to get his uniform. Then George's voice boomed from the bar. He had come back.

Chris took a deep breath; he better got it over with right away.

"What is it with you and my granddaughter, Chris?" George wanted the confrontation and yet hypocritically pretended that he had to clarify something first? What a hound! But he could pretend as well.

"You don't like that Madeline prefers square dancing to the dance circle. I know. Shall I talk her out of it?"

"Either Madeline stays out of square dancing or we find another caller."

"Do you think you're doing Madeline a favor?" To remain dispassionate, Chris sought his salvation in polite distance.

George became pale with anger; he clenched his fists. "She hugged you!"

He nodded slowly. "We like each other."

"Don't you dare! I'll press charges, you... you... playboy."

"What for, Mr. Lagrange? I know my responsibility."

"Madeline is a child. She doesn't know what's good for her."

"If you know better, I'm sure you'll be able to convince her." Chris slipped into his jacket. He wouldn't engage in a fight where he could only get the short end of the stick.

But he would be vigilant. Lagrange could do anything.

Madeline would better stay away from square dancing for now. But he couldn't talk to her about it without revealing his deep feelings for her. And then she wouldn't be willing to keep her distance. This girl knew no compromise.

It was enough to think of her, that an unbridled longing burned in him to hold her in his arms, to feel her opening up to him, to meet him eagerly.

11

"Before or afterwards?", Madeline mailed before the next practice session. She was hoping for afterwards. Then she would have Chris to herself. All she had to do was get rid of Marga before he took her home. Madeline turned off the computer. She just wouldn't look at the mails before she left the house. Then she could pretend she didn't know anything and he would practice with her afterwards.

But Chris thwarted her calculation by disappearing to his shift immediately after the session. And that after he'd continually had something to correct that night. The next time he did the same; and both times he hadn't even responded to her mail.

She decided to confront him. If he really had night shifts, he'd be home by day. After school, she went to his place instead of going home.

He opened the apartment door without asking who was there. Barefoot, his hair tousled, a five o'clock shadow on his chin and naked under a kimono that went only to half of his thighs: He obviously just got out of bed. At least he hadn't lied to her.

He stared at her.

"May I come in?" He looked mouth-watering. The dark trace of fine hair on his naked chest tempted her to trace it with her fingers. At that thought her breath accelerated.

He was still staring at her, but his eyes were starting to

sparkle. He knew what she was thinking. And he thought the same.

Now or never! She stepped up to him and as he took a half step back to bring distance between them, she was in his apartment.

Right across the hallway, the door to his bedroom stood wide open. It was big, but his bed was so narrow that he certainly almost always slept alone in it.

Madeline grabbed him by the shoulder. "What's happened? Why aren't you practicing with me anymore? Why don't you answer my mails?"

His smile seemed rather pathetic. "You don't need it."

She squinted her eyes. "In what respect?" Hah! The flash in his eyes proved that he knew exactly what she meant.

She leaned into him. He kept his hands outstretched so he wouldn't touch her. "And I thought..." She raised her face to him. "Chris, I love you."

For a moment, he stood completely still. At least, he didn't make fun of her.

But he pushed her away. "Madeline, be reasonable."

"I'm not even going to consider it!" She stomped her foot. "Truly, I didn't think you were such a coward."

Chris gritted his teeth. There would be only one way to prove her wrong. If he didn't want to, he'd have to put up with it.

"Your grandfather's about to blow up the whole square dance group."

"That's not for him alone to decide!" She squinted her eyes to hold back the tears. "If you really want something..." She turned abruptly and left. It echoed all over the house as she slammed the door.

12

After that, Madeline didn't come to practice. Without notification. She hadn't contacted Hinnerk either. That was what Chris wanted to achieve to protect the group. And himself. But she was missing – he missed her.

The dancers' piercing stares lay on him the entire time; everyone was only half in it. He had a guilty conscience. To the group. But even more to Madeline. But she'd get over it. As for himself, however, he was not so sure.

Shortly before the end of practice George's voice reached them in the hall. As if on command, everyone stopped dancing.

Chris repeated his call. The dancers were still standing motionless. "Do you need an explanation?"

"Yes," Hinnerk replied. "What's wrong with you and Madeline?"

"I guess it's none of your business."

"Looks like everyone's business." Micky put his fists on his hips and came one step closer.

Instinctively Chris raised his shoulders. "Madeline didn't come today. So what? You've all been missing at some point."

"Not without calling off." Tanja raised her hand to cut off any objection. "We do realize George doesn't like that Madeline is more into square dancing. But she didn't come to the dance circle either."

"See? It has nothing to do with us. She will have forgotten time over her school assignments. Or the day."

Hinnerk took his cell out of his pocket. "We'll ask her."

Chris shrugged, pretending indifference. Madeline would have no answer for Hinnerk; she was far too proud and stubborn.

Suddenly George stood in the doorway. "Madeline's not here today?" Was that hypocritical or did he really not know?

"The *Abitur* is approaching," Norbert explained. "She has always said it comes first."

Carola smirked. "I'm glad you care that she's dancing at least something."

George grunted. "That's not why I came. We need to talk."

"Good," said Lydia Aydemir. "We'll all stay on." She turned around. "Can we move on now, Chris?" As if it hadn't been the group itself that interrupted the dance.

Chris repeated his last call once more.

They danced flawlessly. George watched them and they all sensed there was something threatening their group.

Then Chris switched off the stereo. Everyone remained in their positions and turned their attention to George as if he were a juror. Which he probably was right now.

"I already said the other day: You guys are good." He squeezed his eyebrows together and looked at Chris. "We should give you the opportunity to ensure regular practice."

"We do practice regularly," Carola protested loudly.

"Well, yeah." George now also squinted his eyes. "But it goes back and forth with the schedule. Thus also for Marga and the tournament groups the organization is very difficult." As if something had changed with their two weekly dates in the last two years.

"What are you up to? Make sure Chris can reorganize his shifts?"

"I've been asking around. The club will hire a new caller for you."

Chris dropped his jaw. He had guessed that George was up to something like that; but that he was so open about it... The man was anything but afraid of conflict.

Norbert grinned broadly. "I didn't know the club would appreciate us so much!" His gaze went round. He must have been calculating how much maneuvering space the group had. Much, Chris was sure of that. "But you needn't bother. We couldn't have a better caller than Chris."

"It's too much trouble." George suddenly sounded defensive. Chris tried to hide his amusement.

"We've settled in with his shifts," Micky replied. "Once the group, once free practice; no problem." He smirked. "Hinnerk with his missions abroad is more of a problem than Chris."

"A new man? You need more replacement dancers?" Had Micky managed to get George off the subject? "Then you will soon have difficulties in keeping the group." Now he prophesied the end of the group?

Carola laughed. "What's on your mind, George? First you butter us up, now you're questioning everything?"

George's face turned red. As usual, the girl knew no finesse; but here it was useful. Chris began to have thievish fun watching George beat time.

"I'm not questioning anything." A clear statement; they could pin him down on it. "The club wants to lead you to more success." They could pin him down on that, too. Triumph flashed on Norbert's face.

"If you want to do something for us: We need Madeline as a regular dancer soon!" Bettina Hinz stroked her belly. "If she could come to practice regularly, she'd be fit until then."

"Madeline has to take care of her *Abitur.*" George must have felt solid ground under his feet again. "She'll know how much leisure she can afford."

Tanja opened her mouth; certainly to come back with her own school days at the *Coliège Français.*

Chris raised his hand to fend her off. Arguing with George was a waste of time. That guy had completely different intentions.

"He's right," he said instead. The square dancers stared at him dumbfounded. "We'd better talk to Madeline about it." He smiled at George as nicely as he still managed. "George has nothing to say to her."

George's face reddened even more. He could not fight this blatant slap without making a fool of himself. The others were smirking.

"Well, that settles that." Tanja hung her bag over her shoulder. "I also have to cram for next week's exams." She grimaced. "Statics; endlessly mathematics."

The group dissolved, completely against all habits, without a chat at the bar. Chris wondered what the old man would cook up next.

13

Three days later Chris knew: He got a registered letter with a subpoena. During his interrogation at the station, Chris heard Madeline raging outside as she made clear that nothing had happened between them. It was ridiculous; of course.

But the next time he came to practice, George intercepted him at the entrance. He made a worried face, as if he had something to regret. "I'm sorry, Chris. But we can't keep you on the job as long as the allegation against you isn't cleared. If word gets around..." George would certainly see to that. "Several of the girls are minors: our responsibility to their families..."

Chris left him without a word. He should see to it himself how he explained that to the square dancers.

He wasn't even down the stairs when his cell rang. It was Norbert. "Chris, please wait for us! We'll come to the pub in a second."

Now he would have to tell the group everything so they could realize what George was really up to. He would have liked to avoid exposing Madeline's grandfather that much — but ultimately it wasn't his problem whether George could retain his position on the board or not. The man was simply too old to understand the world.

The square dancers entered the pub with grim miens. They put several tables together and Norbert pulled Chris onto the chair next to him.

"I just got off the phone with the chairman of the *'Berlin Bears'*. They'll take us all in anytime." He grinned broadly. "All we have to do is bring our own caller if we want to keep dancing as an own group."

"You guys are planning to leave the club?"

Tanja rubbed her finger over the edge of her glass and made it sing. She stared at it as she spoke. "Oh, no; that would be too darn stupid. Axel would be pissed off. And our parents would certainly not appreciate to pay my dues for two clubs." She looked up. "It's more about George wanting to get rid of us."

"He always has!" Hinnerk grunted. "Now he has a pretext."

"But Werner won't want to do without us. After all, he knows how much our performances bring to the club." Andrea Falshagen never said anything in this group. Her sudden verve was impressive.

"I don't work with any other caller, Chris." Micky nodded emphatically. "None of us."

Chris looked at Sonja Kramer and Karen Wächter. "George will inform your parents about the charges. Then the group will be untenable."

"You mean our parents will forbid us to keep dancing with you?" Sonja giggled. "You don't know our parents very well! They have faith in us."

"Besides, nobody believes that kind of bullshit." Micky snorted outragedly.

But Hinnerk's gaze was thoughtfully fixed on him. "There's something else behind it. What is it, Chris?"

"Madeline."

"He is capable of such means to get her out of the group?" Carola's eyes sparked anger. "But she's already not dancing with us anymore! What more does he want?"

Chris shook his head. "There's more. I..." What could he say now? Whatever; they were bound to misunderstand. "It's not just about dancing."

Hinnerk's mouth stood open. Then he closed it very audibly and pressed his lips together. The others looked amazed; only Norbert nodded as if he knew.

"I adhere to the rules." Chris slowly emptied his glass. "But still... It's just a difficult situation."

"Which at best concerns Madeline's parents, not George. Is that girl..." Norbert grinned. "She's mighty bold, that girl. Is she hitting on you?"

Chris' face began to heat. "I try to keep her at a distance."

"You can tell!" Hinnerk hissed at him. "You've been mighty nasty to her lately. I was wondering what this was all about." He growled. "That's not a very nice way to behave."

"Yeah? And what do you suggest I do? If I'm not keeping her away from me, then..." Chris clenched his fingers around the glass.

"You need to come clean with her. She is just getting false hopes." Hinnerk was becoming more and more upset.

Tanja laughed in amusement. "I'm sure she doesn't." She raised her eyebrows as she saw Hinnerks bewildered look. "I'm saying Madeline's hopes aren't that wrong." She looked from one to the other and grinned ever more. "Just look at Chris. This is what a man in love looks like!" For a moment, the triumph over her discovery lingered on her face. But then the grin fell off her. "But how far does that take?"

"How far does that take?" Chris exhaled. "I'm twice her age."

"Oho! If you reflect on that, you really have fallen for her!" Norbert said.

Chris put down his glass and stood abruptly. "I'm on early shift."

Tanja reached for him. "Chris, there are no guarantees in love. No matter how good the circumstances seem to be."

But in this case, the circumstances were bad. Or were they? Madeline's career aspiration also bonded them together, far more than dance. They had dreams they could share... Working abroad, a commitment to *"Médecins Sans Frontières"*...

While Chris was scraping his windscreen with clammy fingers, Hinnerk came out of the pub. After a few steps in the direction of the subway, he turned around. He leaned against the hood and watched him.

Eventually Chris had enough of it. "You're not standing there because you want to freeze your feet off."

"I'm standing here because I don't fancy Bettina as my dance partner."

Chris stopped scraping. "Come again?"

"You heard right. I want to dance with Madeline, not with Bettina. And she knows it – Bettina, I mean."

"And why are you saying that now?"

"For weeks you've been trying to drive Madeline away. That's why she didn't come to practice, not because of her *Abitur*."

"I'd like nothing more than to keep Madeline in the square..." Chris uttered.

"But?"

Chris wiped the ice off the scraper. "No but. Just..." Hinnerk's watchful gaze irritated him more and more. "It's not good." He resumed the ice scraping.

Hinnerk seemed to be waiting for him to keep talking. But Chris was just thoroughly scraping his windshield.

"Are you serious about her?"

Chris looked up. "What do you mean?"

"I fell for Madeline, too. She's such a... a marvelous girl."

Hinnerk's face darkened. "That's why I won't let you bully her."

Chris shook his head. "I don't bully anyone. Especially not Madeline."

"What you're passing over with the other girls with a wink, you're chalking up against her!"

"Just to see her..." Chris' eyes started to sting. He clenched his teeth to not let show that it wasn't because of the cold.

Hinnerk bent over the hood to him and stopped his ice scraping. "You too!"

Chris lowered his head.

Hinnerk yanked at his arm for a moment, then let him go. "For chrissakes! You're a grown man, Chris! Tell her what's going on! Talk to her, but don't drive her away. Don't make her unhappy."

"And what shall I tell her? In your opinion?" He opened the car door at the back and threw the ice scraper onto the floor. "Get in, Hinnerk. I'll give you a ride. Otherwise you'll freeze to death."

"Thanks, but no thanks; wrong direction." Hinnerk stepped back from the car and raised his hand in greeting. Chris watched him until he disappeared at the subway station. He' d be well suited to Madeline. The mere thought of Hinnerk dancing with her was hurting that it was almost unbearable. If he wasn't committed to the group, he'd pack up and leave. Forget all this Berlin. Forget Madeline.

14

Madeline was still raging when her grandparents came to dinner. "Grandpa, did you think you could get away with that? Or I wouldn't know? What you've done is downright indecent!"

Bruno was flabbergasted. "How do you talk to Grandpa?"

Konstanze stepped up behind Madeline: "She's right. It's outrageous what George has done."

"But what on earth happened?"

"I guess it's called slander. Stalking!" Madeline pushed Konstanze aside and rushed out. It might not be fair that she left her to explain, but she would scratch Grandpa's eyes out if he even opened his mouth.

In the hallway she stood undecided for a moment. Then she put on her boots and coat and left the house.

It was snowing again and the air was clear and fresh. She trotted off and jogged around the block once. When she returned to their front door, the grandparents' Passat was still there; of course – they had come for dinner.

And had to have a talk.

Despite the thick boots her feet had become cold and her face was burning. But there was no guarantee that Bruno would allow her to retreat to her room. She pulled her scarf higher over her face and walked on.

Then suddenly she stood in front of the house where Chris lived. But she couldn't just go to his apartment; if someone was watching! Freezing, she stomped up and down.

Grandpa could have hired a private investigator; she wouldn't put it past him. He didn't shy away from anything. Across the street, many windows were brightly lit: someone could be lurking behind a curtain. But wouldn't she have to see him then? Or was there someone in Chris' stairwell?... She had decidedly too much imagination.

She kept walking back and forth, always to the next intersection now. Meanwhile the cold crept under her skirt. It must have been twenty degrees below zero. At least. She hadn't taken any money with her; so she couldn't warm up anywhere in a pub and cabs didn't operate around here.

She looked about once more. No one was on the street. And if someone saw her enter – how would they know she went to Chris? If they even recognized her with her covered face.

She rang the doorbell. No door buzzer sounded and the intercom remained mute. What if he wasn't home?

She began working the bell bar; so early in the evening one of the neighbors would surely open. Finally, the intercom cracked and a husky woman's voice came up.

"I have an important message for Mr. Rinehart," Madeline lied. "May I put it in his letterbox?"

First there came a grumbling, then the door opener buzzed.

Relieved, Madeline pushed the door open. Cozy warmth welcomed her.

And now, what was she doing here? Chris obviously wasn't home. She sat on the stairs next to the radiator and took off her gloves to warm her fingers on the heater. First of all, unfreeze; then it would be late enough to escape her grandparents when she got home.

The warmth made her sleepy. She leaned against the radiator and dozed. She still had homework to do when she got back. In her thoughts she phrased the first sentences for an essay on the politics of the OAS. Hopefully she wouldn't forget them.

She startled when the front door opened. For a moment Chris stared at her in disbelief. "Madeline!" With two quick steps he stood in front of her and pulled her up.

Moisture shimmered on his lashes; snow thawed off his shoulders. The biting smell of smoke mingled with the smell of his aftershave and he had a large bruise on his face.

Madeline reached out for it. "You've had an accident!"

He laughed hoarsely. "Just a scratch. A beam I couldn't avoid fast enough."

"Your work is dangerous." She sounded downright panicky; how unseemly.

***

Chris heard the panic in her voice. How long had she waited for him? She knew his shifts – had she been scared for him? His throat became tight with emotion.

He took her hand off his face and breathed a kiss on her palm. "You worry about me?"

She needn't answer; her gaze said it all. That girl was simply incredible. He closed his eyes for a moment to get his feelings under control.

She took the opportunity, draw herself up and kissed him. Demanding, she pressed her tongue between his lips; he yielded and let her in.

He grabbed her by the shoulders and pressed her to himself. But their thick coats prevented their bodies from touching and then all of a sudden he couldn't stand it anymore. He pushed his hand under her hood, found the edge of the sweater and trailed her collarbone with his fingertips.

Madeline replied with a murmur that came from deep down her throat and excited him immensely.

Breathing heavily, he broke free from her kiss. "I'll take you home."

Madeline shook. "I'm cold. I'm completely frozen."

He nodded. "I'm not surprised."

"Can't I first warm up at your place?" Her eyes were glittering; she had ulterior motives. What was she thinking? That she could seduce him? She was probably right.

"No!" He grabbed her by her hand. "You belong in bed with a hot-water bottle. At home." As she pouted, he narrowed his eyes and fled into an angry admonition. "How are you gonna get something in your head if you're too sick to study?"

That must have helped, because she nodded acquiescently. "Maybe you're right."

He took her by the shoulder and put the hood back over her hair. "Come on, it's still warm in my car."

Madeline hid in her coat and shoved her hands under her armpits as she walked beside him to the front door. She had lowered her head and didn't speak another word until he stopped in front of her parents' house.

She looked around; then she pointed to one of the cars half snowed in. "My grandparents are still here." She sighed and reached for the door handle. But then she turned around and gave him a quick kiss on the cheek. "Night, Chris. Next time I'll come again to practice."

Except there was no practice right now.

Before she reached the front door, it was opened. The massive outline of George stood in the frame.

Sighing, Chris started the engine again.

15

Without a word, Madeline walked past George into the house. He watched her as she took off her boots and coat in the hallway.

"Where have you been?"

She slid her lower lip out. "Take a walk."

"In this weather!"

Madeline shrugged, hung the soaked coat over a hanger and carried it into the bathroom.

He actually followed her. "Through the kitchen window I saw you getting out of Chris' car. You call that walking?"

"That's none of your business, Grandpa!" She clenched her fists to control her anger. "You have nothing to say to me!"

"Since this concerns club matters, I am responsible for you." He was getting loud. "I won't let some runaway American guy ruin my club's reputation."

His club! When had he become so self-serving? Madeline glared at him. It was none of his business what Chris did in his off time.

She took the hair dryer out of the mirror cabinet and sat on the edge of the bathtub to dry her hair. On the hottest level, the hairdryer was so loud that he would have to scream to make himself heard.

He watched her for a moment, then he turned around and went back to the kitchen.

Madeline took her time. When her hair was dry, she brushed it extensively and finally braided it into a thick plait. Then she removed the melted mascara and creamed her cheeks reddened by the cold. Her lips were chapped; thus it was not apparent that she had been kissed. She considered her reflection with a shake of her head. She hadn't been kissed; she had kissed.

Her dawdling was of no use. Grandpa seemed determined to wait until she emerged from the bathroom. Maybe it hadn't even been smart to leave him alone with the others. She straightened her shoulders and left the bathroom. In the hallway she exchanged her house shoes for slippers with high heels to look even taller.

Konstanze stood next to the stove and poured water on a herbal tea. "You can use something hot now." In her right hand still the kettle, she pushed a cup to Madeline. All this was a wordless message that she was on her side as always.

Madeline took a spoon and honey from the closet. "You're a sweetheart, *Maman*." She placed herself next to her as she slowly slurped the hot tea. A united front against Grandpa. "Have you left any food?"

Konstanze pointed to the refrigerator. "But you have to warm it up on your own."

"Sure thing."

Grandpa looked back and forth between Bruno and Konstanze and seemed busy exploring the situation; but he said nothing. Had Konstanze succeeded in getting Bruno on their side?

After the grandparents left, Konstanze filled a plate with vegetables and meat and put it in the microwave.

Bruno reached into the drawer and took out the cutlery. "What did you really do?"

Madeline was tempted to tell him anything, but Konstanze

raised her eyebrows in warning. "I've been jogging. And then I was too cold to walk all the way back home." Now however, she hesitated for a moment. "I know where the caller of the square dance group lives. So I just let him drive me home."

"Nothing more?" Bruno was still suspicious; indeed, he was right.

Madeline sighed. "If it had been up to me..."

Konstanze's gaze told her that she should better confess to Bruno.

"I love him!" Tears came to her eyes. "But he... I don't know. He turned me down. Once again."

"Once again?" Bruno got loud. "You mean you threw yourself at him?"

"I was sure..." A sob made her stutter. "Chris says he's my coach and I'm too young. Yet..."

"He acts wisely, child," said Konstanze. "Can't you see you're putting him in a hell of a mess? Your grandfather knows no bounds."

"How old is he, this Chris?" Bruno, very practical.

Madeline raised her shoulders. "I don't know. I don't care either."

Bruno narrowed his eyes. "Much older then. And what kind of guy is he?"

"Papa! You interrogate me like he's a marriage candidate."

"Isn't he? ... If you were serious..."

"He works with the fire department, Bruno. Your father told me." Konstanze smiled and she suddenly seemed amused. "Perhaps he has more in common with Madeline than dancing. He's a medic."

"He has a paramedic qualification," Madeline added.

Bruno reached for his wine glass and emptied the bottle into it. Distraction or time to think? "He certainly seems to be a responsible person." He reached for Madeline's hand and squeezed it: "You still won't go after him. He'll tell you if he's interested in you."

"I..."

Bruno interrupted her with a brusque movement. "Don't make a laughing stock of yourself. Besides... He would rather despise you." His gaze went to Konstanze. "Love works differently."

"Enough now; eat, child." Konstanze took the plate out of the microwave. "You can come to us with anything; you know that, don't you?"

Madeline nodded with her mouth full. It was enough for this evening. Maybe Grandpa wouldn't say anything anymore either; now, after seeing that he was standing alone.

16

Eighteen!

Grandpa should only dare to meddle with her again. Even though he didn't need to anymore. The club had brought Chris back and resumed the square dance, but because of Bruno's admonitions Madeline had not gone to practice after all. Chris knew how to reach her if he cared about it.

Instead, she had met Hinnerk for the dance circle the evening before her birthday. It had been nice with him and repeating the dance steps made a lot of sense. She had actually some forgotten already. Which, of course, was completely contrary to the purpose of the drill.

Grandpa had been sitting at the bar like every Friday and greeted her downright exuberantly. Did he think she'd come back regularly now? Probably. Full of vindictiveness she had refrained from correcting his error.

Tanja came with Hinnerk in tow to the pizzeria where Madeline celebrated her birthday. Each of them held an oversized package in their hands. The size was fake: the way they were carrying them meant they were very light. Grinning, she took them and placed them with the other ones at the window front.

Tanja sat with the people from the *Collège Français*, whom she still knew at least by sight.

Hinnerk remained standing next to Madeline. "I have to leave straight away for the airport." He smiled sparingly and tugged on a strand of her hair. "But of course I couldn't fail to come and congratulate." His gaze became expectant. "Eighteen. What are you going to do with your new freedom?"

"What do you mean?"

He looked at her sharply. "If you don't know..." Then the wary expression disappeared from his gaze. "I'll be back for the Carnival ball. I'm not gonna miss our date."

What kind of date? It took a minute, then it dawned on her what he was talking about. "I don't know..." She half turned away. "Actually, I've not much to do with the club anymore."

"Oh, come on! It's good practice. That's what you learned to dance for eventually."

Suspiciously, she frowned. "Why do you care so much?"

"Because I care about you. You know that, don't you?" Indeed. But she didn't want to raise hopes, which she then had to disappoint. He didn't deserve that.

He gave her a nudge at the nose. "So hard to decide?"

"Oh Hinnerk; I care about you too. But..."

"I could misunderstand? I don't. But at least you could give me a chance."

"Another one?" she uttered. It was meant to be funny.

"Have I ever had one?" His voice was hoarse; she had hurt him.

She hesitated for a moment, then shook her head. "I don't know. Don't think so."

"Then I have no hope of getting one now." He smiled again, although he must have been disappointed. "But we can have a nice evening. In all friendship." He looked at her pleadingly.

"All right. I'm coming." She couldn't refuse him that after all. "But will you find me among all those masks?"

He snorted. "Almost nobody wears a mask at the club's balls. The Berlin people don't know how to celebrate Carnival."

"I'll still be wearing a mask," she declared resolutely.

In view of her vehemence, exuberance appeared in the corners of his eyes. But she didn't mean it as a joke. Would it be enough to hide from Chris?

"I will recognize you. Because I'm gonna give you the mask." Hinnerk's usual cheerfulness had returned. "I'll bring you one. From Bali or something. At airports in Asia they sell all sorts of things."

A mask from Bali, that would be just the thing!

It looked frightening. Hinnerk brought her the mask two days before the ball, just after landing. In keeping with the ball's motto, Madeline had chosen a chequered Biedermeier dress with ham sleeves, but when she saw the mask, she changed her plan. It took something martial to go with it.

At such short notice the costume rental offered her only the choice between a vampire costume with fluttering sleeves, which should probably represent the wings, and a pirate costume, which was actually intended for a man. At the fitting, the pirate costume hung on her as if on a scarecrow; she took it anyway.

In the large club hall, Gaston Berraque, a music college student, alternated with a small combo that could play not only jazz but also the usual ballroom dances. In the second hall, the music came out of the can, which was indicative of the importance of disco dances within the club. The kids' pleasure was further somewhat diminished by the fact that the disco sound was not allowed to disturb the dancers next door. At least they had a DJ – Chris, who consistently spoke English that evening to set the program clearly apart from that of the older club members.

George inexorably pushed Madeline into the dance hall for the "adults", as he called it. It was exactly as she had feared: Most of the guests were rather lovelessly dressed up; some not at all.

Marga had gone to great lengths, decorating the tables with serpentine streamers and confetti and hanging lampions across the hall on colourfully wrapped ropes. But that was all that gave the hall a touch of Carnival. On all tables lay several short pencils, which even George stared at in amazement.

Her grandparents were unmasked – which meant that also her mask was worthless. Everyone could imagine who she was. Hopefully Hinnerk showed up soon and rescued her from this ghastly atmosphere. On the other hand – Chris was next door. If she appeared there together with Hinnerk, he too would probably recognize her despite her fancy mask.

Marga were going through the rows of tables – handing out dance cards to the ladies. She seemed to enjoy herself quite deliciously with her idea. "That's in style with the ball's motto" – which hardly anyone had adhered to. But no one dared refuse to receive a dance card. Marga had them made entirely according to traditional patterns: On the outside the logo of the club and space for the name of the card's owner. Inside all pieces of music indicating dance, title and composer and below a line for registering the dance partners.

Of course everyone and sundry was coming to greet George. When the first of the gentlemen asked Madeline if she had a dance card, she said no. George contradicted her angrily and she had to grant the gentleman an entry.

But when Robert Merck was heading for her, she quickly stroked out several dances. "My partner hasn't arrived yet. That complicates it now a little."

He smiled smugly. "If you had come with me, I would not have stood you up."

"Hinnerk didn't stand me up! He works." But for a moment she wasn't so sure of it. Hinnerk had been weird when he brought her the mask. And when she had asked him to pick her up, he had dodged it with a flimsy justification.

As she hesitated to give Robert her dance card, George looked at her most indignantly. He was already opening his mouth to say something; at that Friederike put her hand on his arm and restrained him.

Nice prospects! If only she'd stayed home. With a quiet growl Madeline handed Robert her dance card. But when he wanted to sign up for a second dance, she quickly ripped it out of his hand. Robert Merck of all people. "You have no monopoly on me!"

"Oh, really? Hinnerk maybe? Did you cross out all the dances for him?"

Madeline jumped up, grabbed her purse and yanked the mask off her face. "Leave me alone!" Her gaze at George, she tore the dance card into small shreds. He should just dare to say something about it. "Who had this stupid idea?" She flicked the shreds of paper onto the floor.

George had turned red and at Robert's temple a vein was visibly throbbing. But nobody said anything; they didn't want to create a scene.

"You don't have to drive me home, Grandpa. I'll get a cab."

Why wasn't Hinnerk here yet? The thought that she could not rely on him made her even more angry. She grabbed her mask and left. With a deliberately loud bang she slammed the hall door behind her.

When she opened the door to the stairwell, she bumped into Hinnerk.

Grinning, he stopped her. "Is the party already over?"

She hissed at him and he followed her downstairs in

laughter. "I take it you didn't like the ballroom and you said goodbye to your grandparents."

She hissed again.

Hinnerk reached for her hand and whirled her around on the landing. "Wonderful. That's the way it should be!"

"What? Have you gone nuts?" She tried to break free, but he wrapped his arm firmly around her shoulders.

"Come on! Now you can have a good time." He pushed her back up the stairs.

She was too perplexed to resist. "What are you doing?"

"I've been waiting for you here. I had a feeling you wouldn't stand it for long. We'll dance at the disco!"

At that she started again pulling at him to get free. "Oh, no! I'm not going in there. Chris serves as the DJ!"

"Put your mask on. He won't recognize you."

Of that she was not sure at all. She closed her eyes. "I don't want to!"

"We have a date; have you forgotten?"

"Half an hour ago." She snorted in annoyance.

"You think? Did we set a time?" No, they hadn't. Had that been intentional? "You could have expected Chris to be there."

"No!" She kicked at him; he should finally let her go. "He's square dancing."

"Do you think he doesn't go to a disco anymore? Too old?"

"Chris isn't too old!" Why did she say that?

"Just come on!" Hinnerk pushed her through the front door over to the bar. He had Marga give him two glasses of Prosecco and toasted with Madeline. "To making the rest of the evening better than the beginning."

She put down her glass without drinking, and his nose crinkled in amusement.

He pulled a mask out of his pocket and took off his coat. "Off to battle!"

What battle? Again she suspected he was up to something. She took her glass and emptied it hastily.

Hinnerk opened the door to the disco hall and Marusha's "Snow in July" was blaring down the hallway. They slipped in quickly. In the dimmed light, the dancers were hardly more than shadows moving against the light.

Chris had turned his head towards them. The light that fell through the open door must have attracted his attention. Was he staring at her?

Flustered, Madeline shook her head. She was not recognizable under her mask and the oversized costume hid her female forms; even more so in this darkness. Still, she had goose bumps running down her spine.

Chris wore a simple Venetian half mask that seemed to emphasize the glitter in his eyes.

"What are you waiting for?" Hinnerk cried in her ear. He pulled her onto the dance floor.

Madeline closed her eyes and let herself fall into the rhythm of the music. But she could still feel Chris' gaze. Unwavering. Questioning. Urging.

After two fast pieces came a blues and Hinnerk drew her to him. "Better here than next door, isn't it?" He was hot from dancing and his heat burned through her costume. Suddenly he was too close for her comfort and she tried to distance herself from him. She now was dancing with her eyes open and at the next spin her gaze crossed that of Chris. He actually was looking at her unwaveringly.

"Chris recognized me. Why?"

"The way you move?" Hinnerk started humming the melody. He appeared like a content cat.

What was going on here? Meanwhile, she suspected him of having shown Chris the Balinese mask before he had brought it to her. It wouldn't even have been a detour.

The song was over and she broke free. "I feel hot. Let's get a drink."

"Um. Wait here. I'll check things out. Surely you don't want your grandfather to see you." Three steps away from Chris, he let go of her and went to the door. He opened it and looked cautiously outside.

It looked just about silly and Madeline laughed out loud. Aghast, she put her hand to her mouth; but of course too late. Now Chris had certainly recognized her.

Rage rose in her. How foolish to even come here. "What are you laughing at?" she hissed at him. Chris wasn't laughing at all.

"This costume suits you beautifully, Madeline." How could his voice at this volume still sound so soft as if he were caressing her?

Madeline approached automatically. Chris' gaze burned on her and her heartbeat accelerated. She took another step. The stereo separated them, but his aftershave got to her nose. Or was it just the memory of the scent? Never in her life she would have imagined that she would associate a smell with a man. "I'm glad you're having such a good time."

"You don't?" His gaze went to the door where Hinnerk was still standing, then back to her.

Madeline shrugged. "I'm doing Hinnerk a favor." Good thing the mask concealed the blush that rose to her face when she realized how misleading her words were. "He... He doesn't have a regular dance partner because he travels so much."

Chris nodded. "A problem for the square dance group. Since a long time."

Madeline wiggled her toes in discomfort to avoid stepping from one foot to the other. Her gaze also went to the door. "Hinnerk's waiting."

Chris nodded again.

She didn't move. "Shall I..." She cleared her throat. "I could bring you something to drink."

"That would be nice of you."

Nice! She stormed off so she wouldn't explode in front of him.

"The coast is clear!" Hinnerk took her hand and led her to the bar. "Too bad your grandparents know the mask."

She shimmied up on one of the barstools. "They just have to leave me alone. Dance cards!" She snorted. "You really missed something."

Marga brought them a Prosecco and a beer without being asked. Madeline pushed the mask over her hair and wiped the sweat off her forehead with the back of her hand. Then she drank up in one go. "I don't want to know how the samba dancers feel in Rio. They are to swim away in the heat."

Hinnerk laughed. "Maybe after all, they go swimming."

Madeline held out her empty glass to Marga. Marga raised an eyebrow.

"She's eighteen, Marga. You can't stop her anymore."

Marga grumbled a little and then filled up the glass for Madeline. "If you drink so fast, you'll get hiccups."

"Hiccups? Come on, I don't grow anymore." Again she emptied the glass in one go. "That was for thirst. And the next glass I'll drink with devotion." She bent over the counter. "Provided you have another brand. This one here..." She turned up her nose.

"I have mineral water, too." Marga seemed determined to play the watchdog.

"Is Grandpa afraid that the oh so respectable members of the oh so renowned club could get drunk? You have to get drunk for Carnival!" She placed the empty glass to be refilled and turned to Hinnerk. "Or not?"

He shrugged. "I come from northern Germany. There's even less Carnival than here."

Madeline reached for the bottle while Marga poured. "Leave it here; then you don't have to bother with it." She grinned. "It'll be all gone before it gets warm." Cautiously, she touched her cheeks. They suddenly felt a little numb. Funny.

She slid off the bar stool and took her glass. "Come on back and dance." After one step she turned around again. "Marga, I promised Chris I'd bring him something to drink."

Marga looked a little sheepish. Then she took a beer from the fridge and opened it. Hinnerk gave her a look too; but that looked more like triumph, didn't it?

Madeline took the beer bottle in the other hand and strutted back to the hall. Hinnerk was close to her; one hand on her elbow as if to support her. But to open the door, he had to let go of her. The sudden loss of stability confused Madeline and she leaned on him.

Chris had his gaze on her as if he was waiting for her. But the door was really hard to miss. Why didn't Marga have it fixed long ago? She was usually so conscientious.

The beer foamed out of the bottle due to the impetus with which Madeline put it in front of Chris.

"Thank you!" He let the bottle sound against her champagne glass. The CD was finished and Chris turned quickly to start another one.

"Don't we have any real Carnival songs?"

"We have! Next door." Hinnerk stepped up to her. "If you want to go swaying, you have to go back to your grandparents."

She growled. "They think I've been home a long time." She tapped Hinnerks beer bottle with her again empty glass. "Now you forgot to bring the Prosecco."

"Me?" Hinnerk smirked.

"Of course! You may think I'm a monster, but I don't have three arms yet."

"Don't give up hope. Maybe you'll grow another one."

Madeline stared at Hinnerk, stunned for a moment. Did he get nasty now? That went beyond the usual banter. What was wrong with him?

"Better not. Then all the more nobody would want me." She hiccuped suddenly. So it hadn't helped at all that she had been drinking slowly.

"All the more nobody?" Hinnerk's gaze wandered a moment – to Chris? "Aren't those enough who are courting you already?"

"Pah! What am I to do with them? Baby faces. Kids. Green boys." She became aware of the hurt expression in Hinnerk's face and slapped her hand on her mouth in shock. "I don't mean you." The mask pricked her fingers; she dropped her hand.

Out of the corner of her eye she peered at Chris. He was staring unmoved. "And I don't mean you either!" She hiccuped again; this time she was glad about it. The hiccup covered how bitter she sounded.

Chris raised his head a bit higher; his gaze became attentive.

Madeline pushed the mask back onto her hair and pointed her finger at him. "You belong to the other category." The next hiccup interrupted her. Chris didn't move. She went closer, bent halfway over the stereo. "To the others who don't want me." Chris gritted his teeth; the muscles in his cheeks twitched.

The next, even more violent hiccup swayed her hand and she quickly put the glass down, directly on the stereo. Chris reached out. But he didn't go for the glass, he went for her arm.

She suppressed a sob. "You don't want me!"

"Madeline!" His eyes were pleading with her and she wondered what he was pleading for.

"You're picking at me."

"I didn't mean to hurt you." That sounded lame; that wasn't a serious apology.

She glared at him. "But you did it. More than once. And I..." She flashed angry sparks. "Because of you, I let the group down. I can't stand to see you!"

He swallowed heavily.

"Then why are you standing here?" Hinnerk asked from behind.

She whirled around. "Because you made me do it!" She tried to outdo the music. "And yet you knew he was here."

"And you didn't know?" Hinnerk smiled sardonically.

"Madeline." Chris' voice behind her was quiet; strangely enough she heard him anyway. Then she realized the music had stopped.

She turned around again and pointed to the stereo. "You're neglecting your job." He didn't move.

She looked to the side. Of course, they now had everyone's attention. That was just what she needed; if someone told Grandpa.

Another hiccup kept her from speaking. She pressed her hands on the aching diaphragm. And then she felt like she was going to be sick. She swallowed forcefully.

Hinnerk gently pushed her one step aside and stepped up to Chris behind the stereo. "I'll relieve you." He briefly squeezed Chris' arm.

Chris exhaled and approached Madeline, looking firmly at her face. He got so close that her hips touched and a hot wave went up in Madeline. She reached for his shoulder.

Chris' voice got harder. "You've had too much to drink, Madeline!"

She raised her head. "So..." a hiccup... "So what? I'm eighteen now. No one can tell me what to do anymore!" She tried to glare at him challengingly; but she had trouble focusing. Somehow the room revolved around her. Yet she had the certain feeling that a smile was spreading on his face.

"You're eighteen now? Looks like I missed your birthday!"

"You weren't invited." The room revolved faster and she propped herself against him.

Chris embraced her with both arms and led her out of the hall. "Marga, she'll need something for her head."

"My head is impeccable." She let herself slide to the floor at the bar. "Why are you picking at me, Chris?" Tears ran down her face. "I can't bear to see you." She leaned against the wooden panels and closed her eyes. A tear dripped on her hand.

Suddenly Chris sat next to her on the floor and drew her to him. "I love you too." He stroked her hair, then his fingers reached her neck and he stroked her with his thumb while holding her. His mouth was on her cheek and slowly he kissed away one tear at a time.

"I'm twice your age, Madeline. I have no idea how this is gonna work out between us. You're so young and..." He faltered and kissed her gently on the mouth. His tongue played with her lips for a moment, then he tore away. "Who knows if we have a chance. But, heavens, I love you. I want that time with you, no matter how it ends."

Madeline opened her eyes and leaned back far enough to look at him. "We have a lot more in common than just dancing." She wanted to smile, but a new wave of nausea rolled over her. "It won't go too awry. Somehow." She clawed her fingers into his shoulders. "We conquer one day at a time." To hell with the buzz! She was happy.

THE END

About the author

Annemarie Nikolaus began literary writing at the beginning of 2001. After publishing several short stories, her first novel was published in 2005. She now publishes her work independently.

She was born in Hessia/Germany and lived in Northern Italy for 20 years. In 2010, she moved to Auvergne, France with her daughter.

After studying psychology, journalism, politics and history, she worked as a psychotherapist, political advisor, journalist, editor and translator, among others.

If you want to know, when more books are translated into English, then sign up to her newsletter:
http://eepurl.com/bHQtvf

Qindie author: Qindie stands for quality and independence.

Twitter: http://twitter.com/AnneNikolaus

Publications in English:

Magical Stories. Short stories for children. Paperback edition ISBN 9781479157037.

Radiant Hope. Illustrated science fiction story. Paperback edition ISBN 9781484977163.

Past Crimes. Historical crime short stories. Paperback edition ISBN 9781507136744

Silenced. Short thriller. Paperback edition ISBN 9781507176238

Deceased. Short Stories. Paperback edition ISBN 9781507190371.

Aquitaine: The End of a War. *"By The Wayside..."* series. Non-fiction. Paperback edition ISBN 9781507141861

***

Other dance novels:

Back onto the dance floor.

After a serious car accident, Friederike Lagrange had to give up competition dancing and instead made a career as a university professor. Now she dares to return to the dance floor together with a colleague. But when she plans a movie about Baroque dances with the "Lietzensee Dance Club", also her husband wants to dance with her again. Can she solve her dilemma without hurting either of them?

Falling for a movie star.

Tanja Walters' secret love is her square dance partner Micky Hasloff. But when the dancers are hired for a Western, she flirts with the star of the movie, Manolo Rioja. Out of jealousy Micky sabotages the shooting. Only a meeting with Rioja and his wife convinces him that not the star stands in his way, but his own fear. Now does Micky dare to reveal his love to Tanja?

Quick, quick, slow – Lietzensee Dance Club
Dance Novels

The idea for these "Dance Novels" was developed by the author group "Schreibwerk". The stories are set in Germany in a fictitious Berlin dance club during the first decade of this century.

Each book in the series can be read as a stand-alone.

At present, only Annemarie Nikolaus is getting her novels translated. In addition to English, currently available are translations into Italian, Spanish and Greek.

You can find out more (in German) in their blog https://schreibwerk-news.blogspot.com/p/blog-page_28.html

Annemarie's novels:

Die Enkelin. Also in English, Italian, Spanish and Greek.
Zurück aufs Parkett. Also in English and Italian.
Flirt mit einem Star. Also in Italian

Other authors:

Tine Sprandel: **Der Treppensturz** and **Nele.**
Marion Pletzer: **Tanz bei offenen Türen**
Evelyn Sperber-Hummel: **Liebe tanzt Rumba**

www.ingramcontent.com/pod-product-compliance
Lightning Source LLC
Chambersburg PA
CBHW020120310726
48970CB00002B/723